Also by Elizabeth Peters

Silhouette in Scarlet

by Elizabeth Peters

Congdon & Weed, Inc.
New York

Library of Congress Cataloging in Publication Data

Peters, Elizabeth.
Silhouette in scarlet.

I. Title.
PS3563.E747S5   1983   813'.54   82-22174
ISBN 0–86553–072–6
ISBN 0–312–92773–8 (St. Martin's Press)

Published by Congdon & Weed, Inc.
298 Fifth Avenue, New York, N.Y. 10001

Distributed by St. Martin's Press
175 Fifth Avenue, New York, N.Y. 10010

Published simultaneously in Canada by
Thomas Nelson & Sons Limited
81 Curlew Drive, Don Mills, Ontario M3A 2R1

To Paula and Jim

Music I heard with you
was more than music,
And bread I broke with
you was more than bread.

Conrad Aiken

Chapter One

THIS TIME it wasn't my fault.

On several previous occasions I have found myself up to my neck in trouble (and that's pretty high up, because I am almost six feet tall), which might have been avoided if I had displayed a little ladylike discretion. This time, however, I was innocent of everything except stupidity. They say some people attract trouble. I attract people who attract trouble.

Take Herr Professor Dr. Schmidt, for instance. You wouldn't think to look at him that he could be so dangerous. Physically he's a combination of the Wizard of Oz and Santa Claus—short, chubby, disgustingly cute. Intellectually he ranks as one of the world's great historians, respected by all his peers. Emotionally . . . Ah, there's the rub. The nonprofessional parts of Schmidt's brain are permanently frozen at fourteen years of age. He thinks of

1

himself as D'Artagnan, James Bond, Rudolf Rassendyll, Clint Eastwood, and Cyrano de Bergerac, all rolled into one. This mental disability of Schmidt has been partially responsible for propelling me into a number of sticky situations.

Yet Schmidt's profession, which is also mine, sometimes requires its practitioners to enter a world far removed from the ivory towers of academia. He's the director of the National Museum in Munich; I work under him, specializing in art history. Nothing duller or more peaceful than a museum? Tell that to any museum director and listen to him giggle hysterically.

There is a flourishing black market in stolen art objects, from historic gems to great paintings. Murph the Surf, who lifted the Star of India from New York's American Museum of Natural History in 1964, was a veritable amateur compared to modern thieves, who have to contend with closed-circuit television, ultrasonic waves, photoelectric systems, and other science-fiction-type devices. They contend admirably. According to one estimate, seventy-five percent of all museums suffer at least one major theft per year.

Sometimes the stolen masterpieces are held for ransom. Insurance companies don't like to publicize the amounts they shell out for such purposes, but when you consider the prices even second-rate Great Masters are bringing at auction these days, you can see that this branch of the trade pays very well. Other treasures simply vanish. It is believed that criminal organizations such as the Mafia are investing heavily in "hot" art, storing it up like gold and silver coins. And there are private collectors who like to sit in their hidden, air-conditioned vaults gloating over beauty that is theirs alone.

It's no wonder museum directors sleep badly, and worry a lot.

Which has nothing to do with the present case. It wasn't my job, or my tendency to interfere in other people's business that led me astray this time. It was one man. And I should have known better.

ii

It rains a lot in southern Germany. That's why the Bavarian countryside is so lush and green. In bright sunshine Munich is one of the world's gayest and most charming cities. Under dull gray skies it is as dismal as any other town. This spring had been even wetter than usual. (They say that every spring.) As I stood waiting for the bus one evening in late May, I felt that I had seen enough water to last me for a long while. My umbrella had a hole in it, and rain was trickling down the back of my neck. I had stepped in a puddle crossing Tegernsee Allee, and my expensive new Italian sandals were soggy wrecks. A sea of bobbing, shiny-wet umbrellas hemmed me in. Since most Munichers, male and female, are shorter than I am, the streaming hemispheres were almost all on my eye level, and every now and then a spoke raked painfully across the bridge of my nose. Italy, I thought. Capri, with a blue, blue sea splashing onto white sand. Rome, baked umber and sienna by a bright sun. My vacation wasn't due until July. I decided to move it up.

Naturally, the package arrived that evening. Some people have a diabolical sense of timing. Even the weather cooperates with them.

The rest of the mail was the usual dull collection, plus

the weekly letter from my mother, which I wasn't exactly aching to read. It would contain the usual repetitive news about her bridge club and her recipes, plus the usual veiled hints about how I ought to be settling down. My birthday was rapidly approaching—never mind which one—as far as Mom is concerned, every birthday after the twenty-first is a step down the road to hopeless spinsterdom. I kept sending her carefully expurgated descriptions of my social life, but I couldn't expect her to understand why marriage was the last thing I wanted. She and Dad have been like Siamese twins for over forty years.

Before I could read the mail or divest myself of my wet clothes I had to deal with Caesar. He is a souvenir of a former misadventure of mine, in Rome, and there were times when I wished I had brought back a rosary blessed by the Pope or a paperweight shaped like the Colosseum, instead of an oversized, overly affectionate dog. Caesar is a Doberman—at least he looks like a Doberman. Like Schmidt's, his personality doesn't match his appearance. He is slobberingly naive and simpleminded. He likes everybody, including burglars, and he dotes on me. He has cost me a small fortune, not only in food, but in extras, such as housing. Even if I had the heart to confine a horse-sized dog to a small apartment, there wasn't a landlord in the city insane enough to rent to me. So I had a house in the suburbs. The bus ride took almost an hour twice a day.

I let Caesar out and let him in, and fed him, and let him out and dried him off. Then I settled down with the mail and a well-deserved glass of wine.

I opened the package first, noting, with only mild interest, that I was not the first to open it. German customs, I assumed. The stamps were Swedish, the address was in neat block printing, and the return address, required on international parcels, was that of a hotel in Oslo.

Swedish stamps, Oslo address, anonymous printing—
that should have warned me, if there were anything in
this business of premonitions. There isn't. I was still only
mildly curious when I opened the box. But when I saw the
contents—one perfectly shaped crimson rose—my blood
pressure soared.

It had been over a year since I had seen John—almost
three years since the red rose had been mentioned. But I
had good cause to remember it.

"One red rose, once a year." He hadn't said it, I had. At
Leonardo da Vinci Airport, as I was leaving for Munich
and John was leaving for parts unknown, with, as he
quaintly put it, the police of three countries after him.
John was another souvenir of that Roman adventure, and
he had turned out to be even more inconvenient than
Caesar. I had seen him once in the intervening time. We
had spent three days together in Paris. On the third night
he had departed out of the window of the hotel room
while I slept, leaving behind a suitcase full of dirty
clothes, an unpaid hotel bill, and a tender, charming note
of farewell. My fury was not mitigated when I learned,
from a sympathetic but equally infuriated inspector of
the Sûreté, of the reason for his precipitate departure.
They had waited until morning to close in on him, feeling
sure—said the inspector, with a gallant Gallic bow—that
he would be settled for the night.

The police wouldn't tell me what it was he had stolen.
I didn't really want to know.

John is a thief. He specializes in the objects I am paid
to guard and protect—gems, antiques, art objects. He
isn't a very successful thief. He's smart enough, and God
knows he's tricky, but he is also a dedicated coward.
When he hears the heavy footsteps of cops or competi-

tors thundering toward him he drops everything and runs. That may not seem like an attractive quality, but it is actually one of John's more appealing traits. If everybody were as reluctant to inflict or endure pain, there wouldn't be any wars, or muggings of helpless little old ladies.

He has the most atrophied conscience of anyone I know. He also has . . . But perhaps I had better not be too explicit, since I want this book to appeal to a family audience. When he's engaged in what he does so well, one may be momentarily bemused into forgetting his true nature, but one would have to be a damned fool to let him con one at any other time.

I picked up the rose and tried to tear the petals off. As I should have realized, it was one of those silk imitations, quite sturdily constructed. I was reaching for the scissors when I saw something else in the box.

It was a blue imitation leather travel folder containing a plane ticket and a hotel reservation slip. The hotel was in Stockholm. The ticket was to Stockholm. I had a reservation on a plane leaving in ten days' time.

What I had was a bucket of squirming worms. What was he up to this time?

I said it aloud. "What are you up to this time, you dirty dog?" Caesar, sprawled across my feet, took this for a deliberate, undeserved insult. He barked indignantly.

It may have been an omen, who knows? I had both hands on the flimsy paper layers of the ticket, ready to rend it apart. By the time I had reassured Caesar and apologized, I had had a chance to reconsider.

A rose is a rose is a rose, and a ticket is a ticket, and a ticket is a hell of a lot more useful than a rose. My mental excursion into poetry reminded me of another verse, that touching little lyric of Dorothy Parker's, in which she mourns,

> *Why is it no one ever sent me yet*
> *One perfect limousine, do you suppose?*
> *Ah no, it's always just my luck to get*
> *One perfect rose.*

I felt sure John was also familiar with that gem of American literature. A plane ticket doesn't measure up to a limousine, but Dorothy would have preferred it to a rose.

Rain sloshed at the window. I sneezed.

Sweden. The land of my ancestors. (Some of them, anyway.) Roots. Stockholm, the Venice of the North, its canals gleaming under a warm spring sun . . . No, there was too much water in that image. The stately palaces and quaint old streets of Stockholm shining in the warm spring sun . . . As I contemplated the mental picture, the sun shone brighter and brighter. I would use that ticket. And when John showed up, I would spit right in his baby-blue eyes. The Paris hotel bill had set me back almost two hundred bucks.

I looked into the bottom of the box, hoping for something else that had actual cash value—a check (though it would probably bounce) or some trinket stolen from a museum, such as a diamond necklace (though it would undoubtedly be a fake). There was something else in the box—a single sheet of paper. Printed on it, in the same hand as the address on the package, were two words. And these were they: WIELANDIA FABRICA.

I sat staring at the paper for so long that Caesar thought I had passed out and began nervously licking my feet to restore me to consciousness. The only thing that will distract Caesar from this activity, which he enjoys for its own sake, is a bone. I went and got him one, blundering into doorframes and furniture because my eyes were glued to that exasperating message.

I knew what it meant, of course. In case you don't, I will tell you, because it isn't fair to plant clues based on esoteric knowledge. The explicit translation of the phrase should be obvious to anyone with a rudimentary knowledge of Latin—"Wayland's work." But, you ask, who was Wayland?

I first encountered him as Wayland the Smith, in *Puck of Pook's Hill,* when he forged a dark-gray sword with Runes of Prophecy on the blade—a sword that sang when it was pulled from the scabbard. Kipling knew his legendry; he was aware that Wayland had come down in the world since he entered England as a heathen god whose altars reeked with blood and burning. The Norse sagas tell his history; he was a divine smith, like the Roman Vulcan, and, like Vulcan, crippled by malice. When writers wanted to describe a particularly fine piece of craftsmanship they had only to label it WELANDES WEORC. Centuries later, Latin epics were using the same phrase. Wayland's enchanted blades had powers beyond those of mortal steel, and his hilts were of gold, gem-encrusted.

Scandinavia, fabled goldsmith, jewel thief . . . It made an odorous little syllogism, as neat and as crazy as one of Lewis Carroll's exercises in logic. John was on the track of a Viking treasure. Or rather, that is what John wanted me to believe. I didn't believe it. If he really intended to commit grand theft, I was the last person to whom he would broadcast his intentions. The message was just a lure, a juicy chunk of bait—and a fairly ingenious one. My interest was definitely aroused.

I checked the travel folder again. The plane ticket was one-way, the cheapest tourist class. The hotel room had not been paid for in advance, only confirmed. Now I knew I was going to Stockholm, if only for the pleasure of telling that skinflint what I thought of him and his cut-rate romantic gestures.

iii

Schmidt protested volubly when I told him I was taking my vacation. He didn't object to the short notice, like any normal boss. The thing that bothered him was that he would miss his weekly installment of the dirty book I was writing. I had been working on the damned thing for three years. It began as a semi-serious attempt to make some money, but it had become a joke; the manuscript already filled two big cartons, and no end was in sight. I could have wound it up at any point; one merely needs to decide how many times the heroine has to be abducted and assaulted before satiety sets in. But Schmidt was hopelessly hooked on Rosanna's adventures. I kept feeding him chapters like Scheherazade with the sultan.

"But she is hiding in the broom closet while the Huns search the house," he exclaimed. "How will she escape? Did not Attila remark, at the end of chapter four hundred and twenty, 'We have not looked in the broom closet'? This time, surely . . ."

"She won't be raped," I said. "It's against my principles to allow a heroine to be raped."

"What of that night in the perfumed, silk-swathed tent of the Emir Ahmed?"

"That was not rape."

"Ah, so," said Schmidt, like Fu Manchu.

"You'll just have to wait, Schmidt. I'll be back in a couple of weeks."

"Could you not give me a small hint?"

I couldn't. I never know myself what Rosanna is going to do until I sit down at the typewriter. "No," I said firmly. "The new Valerie Valentine is out—it's called *Passion's Burning Lust.* That should hold you for two weeks."

"She is good, but not as good as you," Schmidt said. "She has not your imagination."

He gave me one of his pouts—an elderly baby yearning for his bottle. I shook my head. Schmidt sighed.

"Oh, very well. I hope you enjoy yourself."

"So do I," I said grimly.

"The land of your ancestors," Schmidt mused. "Seeking out your roots—yes, it is very romantic. You will stay at the Grand?"

"Fat chance. It's too expensive."

"But you must stay there. It is very romantic. And very convenient."

He meant it was convenient for him. He'd know how to find me if he started to suffer from withdrawal symptoms. It was a tempting idea, though. The Grand is almost as romantic as Schmidt thinks it is, one of the famous old hotels of Europe. And—needless to say—it was not the hotel where John had booked a room for me.

"Yes," Schmidt insisted. "You will stay at the Grand. The manager is an acquaintance of mine. I will telephone at once."

Oh, well, I thought. Why not? In for a penny, in for a few thousand kronor. I could always move to a cheaper place if I ran short of cash.

It was raining—what else?—the day I left, after depositing Caesar at a hideously expensive kennel. It was—of course—also raining in Stockholm. The plane glided down through soupy gray clouds into a landscape so shrouded in mist I couldn't see a thing. Resignedly I struggled into the raincoat I had brought in the hope that I wouldn't need it.

I had decided to use the plane reservation. I doubted that John would meet me at the airport; he was conceited enough to assume I would trot obediently to the hotel he had selected and sit with folded hands until he condescended to get in touch with me. But with John I could never be certain. I came out of customs in a wary crouch, looking for trouble in the form of a dapper blond crook.

There were a good many fair heads visible, but none had the silver-gilt glimmer of John's. Reassured, I straightened up and went looking for the currency exchange.

I love airports—the bustle and excitement, the air of expectation—people beginning or ending adventures of their own—tearful farewells, smiling reunions. The well-dressed balding man with the expensive briefcase and the frown of concentration—he might be a diplomat on a secret mission to an eastern trouble spot, or a businessman, brooding on the complexities of a billion-dollar deal, or a nervous husband meeting a lady friend in Copenhagen for the weekend and hoping to God his wife wouldn't call the office. (Don't worry about the well-dressed man, you'll never see him again. He's just an example of my imagination at work.)

Nobody was paying any attention to me. You have no idea how great that made me feel. Bavarians are short and stocky and brown-haired. Usually I'm a head taller than any woman in a Munich crowd, taller than most of the men, and my yellow head glares like a beacon. But this place was filled with Swedes—wonderful, tall, blond Swedes. There were at least three females in the vicinity who were my height. I knew then that the trip was going to be a success. Wonderful country! Wonderful people! Roots!

I was so dazzled by this discovery that I didn't mind the fact that I had, as usual, selected the slowest moving of the lines at the currency exchange. Some poor idiot with no idea of what he wanted or how to ask for it was at the counter arguing with the teller; the people ahead of me in line grimaced, muttered, or left to try their luck in another queue. I just stood there admiring the view. Tall, blond people—people like me. I knew how Gulliver felt when he got back from Lilliput.

One man caught my eye, and not only because he was inches taller than his tall countrymen. He had to be a Swede. With a horned helmet on that magnificent thatch of flaxen hair, and a coat of chain mail covering those magnificent shoulders, he'd have been the image of a Viking warrior, like the ones in the books I read when I was a kid. Never mind that the Vikings didn't wear horned helmets; the illustrations in the book had imprinted the image onto my brain. This man even had a long, droopy mustache like the one sported by Leif Eriksson.

He stood sideways to me, reading a newspaper, and was unaware of being observed. I continued to stare, hoping he would look in my direction. Finally he shifted and glanced up. So much for the power of the piercing stare; he didn't look at me. I followed his gaze to discover what was so much more fascinating than me.

Characteristically, John had overdone the disguise just a bit. I guess he was trying to look like a Near Easterner of some variety. He had the build for it—slight, slim, lithe. Now his hair was dark and his complexion was a smooth, pale olive. The little black mustache and the too-well-tailored suit suggested Rudolf Valentino. I might not have recognized him if he hadn't been ignoring me so ostentatiously. As he stared fixedly into the middle distance his profile was turned to me, and the structure of that impeccable outline was unmistakable.

The sight of him brought on an overwhelming flood of emotion—frustrated anger, amusement, contempt, and another feeling, of the sort that Schmidt would probably call "romantic." (By now you should have a pretty good idea of what that word means to Schmidt.) The first emotion predominated. I didn't stop to think, I didn't wonder why he was in disguise; the mere fact that he preferred not to be noticed was reason enough to publicize his presence. I opened my big mouth and yelled, "Hey, John. John Smythe! Hi, there, John."

My voice, at full volume, has been compared with that of Brunhild leading the ride of the Valkyries. John started convulsively. Every head within a thirty-yard radius turned toward me. I waved, I stood on tiptoe, I pointed. The heads turned in John's direction.

A wave of color—sheer rage, I'm sure—darkened his cheek to olive drab. I knew his ability to combine speed of movement with inconspicuousness; one minute he was there, the next he was gone. It seemed to me that there was an odd little eddy of movement around the spot he had vacated—a kind of swirl of bodies.

The man behind me nudged me. The line was moving. I closed up the gap that had opened between me and the person ahead.

I had not the least intention of going after John. What bothered me was the impression that someone else had done just that. Uneasily I contemplated his original location, by a pillar next to the newsstand. It was a logical place for people to meet if they missed one another at the gate or the exit from customs. The crowd seemed thinner now. I tried to recall individual faces and shapes, but to no avail; I had not been paying attention to anyone but John and the Viking. The latter was still there, and he was still thoroughly uninterested in me. Folding his newspaper, he tucked it under his arm and strolled away.

Nudged again, I shuffled forward. It would not have surprised me to learn that someone was following John. Someone usually was—an outraged husband, a policeman, a fellow criminal . . . The list of people who might want to murder or cripple John was infinite. If I felt any guilt about raising the view halloo, my conscience was assuaged when I recalled that he had summoned me to Stockholm, right into the middle of whatever scam he was currently working. No, I didn't feel guilty, I felt like killing the rat myself.

After cashing a traveler's check I headed for the exit. I had intended to take the airport bus into the city, but at the last minute I had a change of heart. Ducking out of the line, I ran like hell and threw myself into a taxi. I got some outraged stares from the people who were ahead of me, but I was past caring about good manners. It had occurred to me that in my anxiety to inconvenience John, I had made a slight mistake. In fingering him, I had also fingered myself.

Chapter Two

IT HAD STOPPED raining by the time the taxi reached the city, but I couldn't enjoy the scenery; I was too busy watching for pursuers. There didn't seem to be any, but it was impossible to be sure; every other car on the road was a cream-colored Saab. The sun made a tentative watery appearance and I decided I was being paranoid. If John had been under surveillance, my uninhibited whoop of greeting must have convinced a watcher that I was unwitting—or vastly unqualified for the role of co-conspirator.

The Grand Hotel is on the waterfront, near where Lake Mälaren meets the Baltic. The weathered green copper of the roof supported half a dozen flagpoles, from which the yellow and blue of the Swedish flag rippled in the breeze. Crimson shades marked the front windows and made a thick red line above the café and restaurant on the ground floor. Lined up at the quay in front of the hotel were some of the low white tourist steamers that ply the inland waterways. Even on a dull day the colors were stunning—clean, vivid colors, red and white and green and blue.

The lobby was filled with a truly international crowd: Japanese businessmen and German tourists, American students and Saudis in flowing robes. It wasn't until after I had been escorted to my room and the bellboy had left that my spirits received a slight check. He had arranged my suitcases in neat alignment on the luggage rack. Prominently displayed were the labels, inscribed in my sprawling hand: "Dr. Victoria Bliss, Grand Hotel, Stockholm."

The cases had been in plain view the whole time I waited in the currency-exchange line, including a good five minutes after I had raucously identified myself as a friend of John Smythe. It had been a waste of time watching for pursuing cars. If anybody wanted me, he knew where to find me.

I don't believe in sitting around hotel rooms when I'm on holiday, but I got out of that one faster than I usually do.

I walked out of the hotel into the glorious sunshine I had yearned for. Gulls soared and swooped, crying hoarsely. A brisk sea breeze ruffled my hair. Waves slapped against the quay. There were boats all over the place—chugging busily along the water, docking, departing, bobbing at anchor. I felt like a kid with a fistful of money staring in the window of a toy store; the whole luscious city was spread out before me, parks and museums and shops and streets and canals.

The tourist water buses looked like fun, but I was tired of sitting. Across the inlet the dignified eighteenth-century facade of the royal palace filled one corner of the little island called Gamla Stan, the Old Town, or the City Between the Bridges—everything in Sweden seems to have several different names.

In the bulging shoulder pack I use in lieu of a purse I had a brochure on Gamla Stan that I had picked up at a travel agency in Munich. Six centuries of history, beginning with the thirteenth; cobbled streets and narrow alleys, medieval doors and baroque portals. . . . I had visited a number of quaint old towns. Southern Germany has lots, complete with medieval ramparts and timbered houses. However, one can never get too much of a good thing. Also, the brochure had contained quite a few advertisements. The famous shop for Swedish shirts; Scandinavian knitwear; crystal from Swedish glassworks; old prints, books, maps; leather, silver, pewter, handwoven rugs, hand-embroidered blouses. . . . I might claim that it was my antiquarian interests that led me to the twisty alleys of Gamla Stan, but if I claimed that I would be lying.

Like similar sections in other cities—Getreidegasse in Salzburg, Georgetown in Washington, D.C., the Via Sistina in Rome—Gamla Stan has become chic and fashionable and very expensive. Many of the shops occupied the ground floors of old buildings. The sculptured stone portals and intricate iron grillwork formed surprisingly pleasant settings for displays of modern Swedish crafts. Pedestrian traffic was slow. People stopped to read guidebooks or stare in shop windows or gathered at corners where itinerant performers played and sang.

I don't know how long I wandered in purposeless content before I gradually realized I wasn't relaxed any longer. Instead of admiring red wooden horses and knit ski caps, I was scanning the crowd, looking for a familiar profile. Instead of enjoying the diversified types strolling with me, I was beginning to feel surrounded and hemmed in. My back tingled with the uneasy sensation of being watched by unfriendly eyes.

It was with an absurd sense of escape that I emerged from the crowded streets into Stortorget, the Great Square of Old Town. I'd seen so many pictures of it, on postcards and travel folders, that it was like an old familiar habitat. Earnest tourists were aiming cameras at number 20, the tall red brick house with its exuberant wedding-cake gable, which is the most popular subject for photographers; it would reappear on screens in a thousand darkened living rooms later that summer while guests tried to muffle their yawns and the host's voice intoned, "Now this one is someplace in Stockholm—or was it Oslo?"

The square was filled with people, but it didn't give me the sense of claustrophobia the streets did. Rows of green slatted benches were flanked by great tubs of red geraniums, and the sun slanting down between the tall houses made the flowers glisten as if freshly painted. I decided my neurotic fancies were due in part to hunger, so I bought some jammy pastries from a shop and sat down on one of the benches where I could see the baroque tower of the Cathedral beyond the Borsen and the slitlike street beside it. When I had finished the pastries I licked strawberry jam off my fingers and continued to sit, staring dreamily at the green-patined curves of the cupola.

I guess my feet did stick out, but he could have avoided them. I didn't see him; I felt an agonizing pain in my left instep and heard a crunch and a thud and a curse as a large object fell flat on the bricks at my feet.

I let out a howl and bent to clutch my foot. He let out a howl and stayed where he was, face down on the ground. He looked just as big prone as he had upright— a fallen Colossus, a toppled Titan.

If the same thing had happened in Denmark, we would have been swarmed over by helpful natives. Swedes don't interfere unless arterial blood is jetting. There were a few murmurs of inquiry and one man took a tentative step toward the recumbent body, but retreated as soon as it heaved itself to hands and knees.

When he turned his head our eyes were on the same level. His weren't blue, as a Viking's ought to be; they were an odd shade of brown, like coffee caramels. Between the bushy brows, the bushier mustache, and the thick hair that had fallen over his forehead, I could see very little of his face. What I could see was bright red, and his eyes glittered like bronze spearpoints.

"Clumsy, careless—" he began. Then his eyebrows rose and disappeared under his hair. "You were at the airport!"

It sounded like an accusation. I half expected him to demand indignantly, "Are you following me?"

"Yes, I was at the airport. So what? I think my foot is broken. Why the hell didn't you look where you were going?"

Still on hands and knees, he gave his head a toss that flung the blond berserker locks away from his eyes. Caesar had a trick like that when he was trying to be cute. I laughed. The Viking staggered to his feet, swayed, swore, and clutched his knee. The woman sitting next to me on the bench picked up her parcels and beat a hasty retreat. It may have been tactful consideration for a wounded fellow creature, but I think she was afraid he was about to fall on her.

He took the vacated seat. We sat in stiff silence for a few seconds while he rubbed his knee and I nursed my foot.

Finally he muttered, "Sorry." His voice was rather light for such a big man, once he had conquered the anger that had deepened it to a growl.

"You should be."

"Let me see."

I caught the edge of the bench as he took my foot onto his lap; but he did it skillfully, without upsetting my balance. A woman of my size does not have small feet. His huge brown fingers reduced my size ten to something as dainty-looking as that of a Chinese maiden.

He returned the foot to me. "There will be a bruise, I am afraid. Perhaps you had better visit a doctor."

"No, it's all right. How about your knee?"

Unconcernedly he rolled up his pants leg. His calf was as big around as the thigh of a normal man, thick with muscle and covered with fine hairs that glowed in the sunlight like the golden nimbus that surrounds the bodies of saints and divine heroes. I was so fascinated by this fabulous anatomical specimen that I didn't get a good look at the wounded knee. I caught only a glimpse of reddened skin before he pushed the fabric down.

"It is not so bad."

"I am glad," I said slowly, "that you did not tear your trousers."

"I too am glad. They were very expensive."

They didn't look expensive. However, that is a relative term, and I didn't feel I knew him well enough to pursue the subject. As I started to rise, he put his hand on my arm.

"You will allow me to buy you—" he said.

"I don't really think—"

"A schnapps. Or something else, if you prefer."

"I don't really—"

"You must allow me."

"Must" was the word. It wasn't an invitation; it was an order, and the weight of the hand on my arm reinforced it.

All at once I was overcome by the most abject feeling of panic. I am—as I have mentioned a time or two—unusually tall. I am also built like my Scandinavian ancestors—big-boned, well-muscled. Wrestling matches with my brothers had toughened me at an early age, and I'd kept in reasonably good physical condition with exercise and diet. Now for the first time in my life I understood how my normal-sized sisters feel when a man grabs them. Small, weak, vulnerable.

My eyes moved from the hand that dwarfed my not inconsiderably muscled arm, up along a couple of yards of coat sleeve, to his face. It was an almost perfect rectangle; the angles of jawbone and cheek were so square that the lower part of his face formed a straight line. His lips were full and healthily pink, bracketed by the luxuriant growth of hair on his lip. His nose rose out of the brush like a sandstone promontory; his eyes, wide-set and slightly protruding, met mine with unblinking sobriety. Every feature was larger than life-sized, but they harmonized perfectly. He was, to summarize, a handsome man with a gorgeous body, the kind of man who could turn a vacation into a memory of the sort little old ladies simper over when they sit rocking on the front porch of the nursing home.

"Thank you," I said.

I could have eluded him if I had wanted to. He didn't take my arm or hold my hand. At times, when the crowds thickened, we had to walk single-file through the narrow streets. He preceded me, explaining solemnly, "I go first because I know the way. You will excuse the rudeness."

The stiff formality of his manner made me smile, and I dismissed that brief moment of panic. I just wasn't accustomed to feeling fragile and feminine, that was my trouble.

It was something of a coincidence that we should run into one another twice in the space of a few hours. However, Stortorget and the Old Town are tops on the lists of most tourists. Even if he had followed me, even if the accident had been premeditated—well, I have my share of vanity. I could think of reasons why a man might force an acquaintance with me, reasons that had nothing to do with John Smythe. When Leif Eriksson bowed me into the doorway of a restaurant that had once been a wealthy merchant's house, I stepped right in.

I had schnapps. I had been meaning to try it anyway.

The alcohol loosened him up a little. He even ventured to ask a personal question.

"Are you, by chance, American?"

I nodded. "And you," I said, with equal gravity, "are, by chance, Swedish?"

"Why do you think so?"

"Because only a Swede would hedge about a simple question like that."

He laughed. It wasn't one of your hearty Norse guffaws, but a prolonged chuckle, as rich and mellow as his speaking voice was light. The mustache added a fascinating dimension to his smile. The ends actually appeared to curl up parallel to his lips. His teeth were big and white, just the dentures to rip into a haunch of raw meat.

"You are unkind to us," he protested. "Why do you have a prejudice against this country?"

"I'm not—I mean, I don't. I'm half Swedish myself. The other half is a mixture—Norwegian, Swiss-German, American Indian, you name it. Like all Americans, I'm a mongrel, and proud of it."

He frowned a little, as if puzzled. Abandoning the problem with a shrug, he announced, "My name is Leif Andersen. And yours?"

I hadn't quite decided whether to give him an alias. The abruptness of the question, and the surprise at hearing a name so close to the one I had imagined for him, took me off my guard.

"Vicky Bliss," I said, mumbling. We shook hands over the schnapps glasses. I felt my bones crunch.

He ordered another round, and asked me what I was doing in Stockholm. I said I was on holiday. I asked him what he was doing in Stockholm. He said he was on holiday. I have had livelier discussions with retired schoolteachers. Unperturbed, I sipped my schnapps and bided my time. Swedish men once had a reputation for reticence and reserve. Presumably customs had changed since the sexual revolution, although most of the enthusiastic comments I had heard about modern mores concerned Swedish women and were, I might add, based more on wishful thinking than on actual experience. It was all irrelevant. If Leif wanted to move in on me with the ponderous deliberation of a brontosaurus plodding toward its mate, I could wait. So long as he moved in. He was the tallest man I had ever met.

Then he said, "You are here alone?"

A slimy little tendril of caution poked out from under the erotic fantasies that had buried my suspicions. He didn't look like a Swedish Jack the Ripper—but then, who does? And he had been at the airport. . . . I lowered my lashes bashfully and remained silent.

"I ask," he explained, "because when I saw you at the airport you were greeting a friend."

"He's no friend of mine." I spoke without hesitation, as I would have denied being intimately acquainted with Hitler. "I thought I recognized someone I knew slightly . . . once . . . a long time ago."

Leif leaned forward and put his elbows on the table. I

caught one of the schnapps glasses as it slid toward the edge.

"I think I can trust you," he muttered.

Oh, damn, damn, damn, I thought. Here we go.

---

ii

The waiter trotted up just then to ask if we wanted anything else. Leif ordered another schnapps. I ordered coffee. I had the feeling I had better keep my wits about me, and I was grateful for the delay, as the waiter hovered, nudging Leif's elbows off the table and lighting the candle enclosed in a stubby ruby glass holder. It wasn't dark outside yet, and wouldn't be for hours, but evidently evening had officially begun. The café was getting lively. In the background a small combo broke out in a disco beat.

As soon as the waiter had left, Leif leaned at me again. Little red flames reflected by his pupils shone diabolically.

Before he could speak, we were interrupted a second time. A man sidled up to us, cleared his throat deprecatingly, and in a soft, barely audible voice made a suggestion. It wasn't a vulgar suggestion, though his manner would have suited a drug peddler or seller of dirty postcards. What he actually said was, "May I make a silhouette of the lady?"

The light was so dim I couldn't make out his features clearly. The most noticeable thing about him was his hair, which was thick and coarse and lifeless, the same dull gray shade as his shabby pullover. Tinted glasses shielded his eyes. Crimson light glinting off the thick lenses gave him the look of a buggy-eyed monster from Arcturus or Aldebaran.

Taking my surprised silence for consent, he pulled out a chair and sat down. From his briefcase he removed a handful of papers and fanned them out on the table.

I know a little bit about a lot of things, most of them utterly useless. I hadn't learned about silhouette cutting from any of my courses, though it can be considered one of the minor arts; I had read about it in an antiques magazine on my last visit home. My mother is a fanatic collector of junk, known in the trade as "collectibles." Silhouettes are among the few things she doesn't collect, possibly because good examples have become very expensive, such as the portrait of Ben Franklin, cut by Major André, or George Washington, by his stepdaughter Nellie Custis. The art had flourished during the nineteenth century, before photography provided a cheap, convenient method of portraiture. I had not realized anyone still practiced it, and I was impressed by the examples the little gray man spread out. The outlined profiles, black on stark white mounts, captured an astonishing degree of individuality.

"For so beautiful a lady I make a special price," the artist murmured. "Twenty kronor—if she will permit me to keep a copy for myself."

Leif shifted position and made grumbling noises. I disregarded them. I wasn't especially anxious to hear what he had to say, and besides, my curiosity was aroused.

"It's a deal," I told the artist.

His tools were the simplest imaginable—a pair of sharp scissors and a sheet of black paper. I gave him a profile, and watched out of the corner of my eye. After one long, measuring survey, he began to cut, the paper turning smoothly in his hands as he clipped, without a pause or a second look at me. It was an astonishing performance, a demonstration of the art in its most difficult and refined form of freehand cutting. Less-skilled cutters worked from a shadow outline or a mechanically produced tracing of the profile. The little gray man was the latest, perhaps the last, practitioner of a unique and dying art form.

After an interval of less than three minutes he gave a grunt of satisfaction, laid the black outline against a piece of thick white cardboard, and held it up.

It was me—I mean, I. I hadn't realized my chin was quite so prominent, but it was unquestionably my chin. He had even managed to suggest the slightly disheveled state of my hair and the presence of the scarf that held it back from my face.

Twenty kronor was dirt cheap for a display like that, but I couldn't resist showing off. "Edouart only charged a shilling," I said with a smile.

The artist had leaned down to open his briefcase. He came up so fast he almost cracked his head on the table.

"You know of Edouart?"

"The greatest freehand cutter of all time, right?"

"Yes, yes, he was the master." His face came alive. The tight, precisely chiseled lips parted eagerly. "I have studied his methods—his manner of holding the scissors, for example. It is necessary to work quickly, very quickly, to capture—"

Leif cleared his throat. "Have you finished?"

The man's face lost its animation. "Yes, of course. I beg pardon. . . ." Hastily dabbing mucilage on the back of the silhouette, he fixed it to the cardboard and gave it to me.

"You cut two at the same time," I said, as he repeated the process with the second portrait.

"By folding the paper one obtains greater stability." He would have said more, but another cough from Leif stopped him. Eyes downcast, he began putting his materials away.

I groped for my purse, which was on the floor by my chair. My fumbling seemed to annoy Leif; he reached in his wallet and counted out twenty SEK. His manner was that of a surly patron tipping a servant. I found it thoroughly offensive, and as the little man rose, I said warmly, "Thank you. It is a wonderful work of art and I'll always treasure it. Will you do me the favor of signing it?"

Leif—unforgivably—laughed. The cutter's face turned a dull red. The signature he produced was an unintelligible scrawl. I thanked him again, profusely. As he walked away, the waiter came with our drinks.

"Has this man annoyed you?" he asked.

"Quite the contrary." I showed him my portrait, and he grinned.

"It is clever. I have not seen such work except in a museum."

"Then the artist is not an employee of the café?" I asked.

"No, no. We allow such people if they do not bother our customers. Most often they are singers or tellers of fortunes. This is original, at least. . . . Do you wish to dine here? We have an excellent smorgasbord."

"Fine," I said. It was a nice little café, very atmospheric, with dark beams and rough stone walls, and I figured I might as well get dinner out of Leif. If he intended to spend the evening pumping me about Sir John Bloody Smythe, the least he could do was pay for my time.

I studied my menu with intense interest, but Leif would not be put off any longer.

"This is not the place for a private conversation," he grumbled.

"I don't go to isolated places with strange men," I said.

Instead of objecting, he nodded approvingly. "Very wise. What I would expect of a lady of your reputation."

"What do you know about my reputation?" I demanded.

"All those who work in my field are acquainted with Dr. Victoria Bliss. You are employed by the National Museum of Munich, and you are an authority on medieval art."

"Well, well," I said. "Do you by any chance know Inspector Feder, of the Munich police? Short, paunchy man with a bald head?"

Leif grinned, baring all his rapacious teeth, and conjuring up a pair of elongated but attractive dimples. "Feder is tall, not short; lean, not paunchy. But he is, I confess, losing his hair."

This accurate description did not cheer me as it should have. I sighed. "What are you, Leif—Interpol, or the Swedish equivalent of the FBI?"

"It is what you would call the Special Branch of Art and Antiquities. You are familiar with our work?"

"I know that many countries have such special departments. The number of crimes involving art objects has necessitated a corps of men with specialized training. But I wasn't aware that Sweden had suffered to that extent. Besides," I added heatedly, "I'm an art historian, not a private eye. And I'm supposed to be on vacation."

"Dr. Bliss. Will you swear to me that you are not presently involved with Al Monkshood?"

"Who?"

"The man you greeted at the terminal."

"You heard me call him John—John Smythe. Maybe," I said hopefully, "we aren't talking about the same person."

"He has as many aliases as hairs on his head," Leif said, grinding his big white teeth. "Smythe is one of them. Yes, we are talking about the same person. Do you expect me to believe that it was by coincidence that you hailed the best art thief in Europe?"

"He isn't all that good," I mused. "Al Monkshood . . . What won't he think of next? Look here, Leif, let's order dinner and get the waiter out of our hair; then I'll tell you what I know. It isn't much."

I am not uninterested in food. A woman of my size needs her nourishment. But I can't remember what we ordered or how it tasted. If I could have gotten my hands on John Smythe, AKA Al Monkshood, I would have squeezed his neck till his face turned puce.

We sat in silence until the waiter had brought our dinner. The silhouette cutter was still circulating; head bent over his work, he was reproducing the far from symmetrical features of a chubby Italian paterfamilias several tables away.

Our own table wasn't very big. By the time the waiter finished fussing over the arrangement of the dishes, Leif was simmering with frustration. He kept dropping things—napkins, forks, menus—and diving under the table to retrieve them. His face was flushed with exertion by the time the waiter had finished.

"Well, then, speak," he demanded.

"Okay, okay. I met Sir John Smythe, as he called himself, in Rome several years ago. I know the title is a fake, and I presume the name is, too, though he told me John was his real first name. He was mixed up in a scheme to copy famous antique jewels and steal the originals. But," I said, "if you're familiar with his career, you probably know the details."

"Natürlich," Leif said impatiently.

"Then you know the scam didn't succeed—thanks in large part to me." Leif gave me a raised eyebrow, but modesty is not a virtue I cultivate. I went on, "Smythe and I were allies at one point because certain developments threatened him as well as me. I can assure you, I have no fond memories of the man and no reason to seek him out. I'd just as soon cohabit with a rattlesnake."

I applied myself to my meal—whatever it was. "That is all?" Leif demanded.

"That is all." It was all he was going to get. What I had told him was public knowledge—at least it was information available to any police officer. My private dealings with John were none of Leif's business.

"Why did you choose Sweden for your holiday?" he asked.

"Why not? It's the land of my ancestors."

"You have kin here?"

"Probably. . . . Leif, I've tried to be cooperative, but I am terribly, terribly sick of Smythe-Monkshood and everything to do with him. There is nothing else I can tell you that could be of use to you."

That wasn't strictly true, but there were several good reasons for neglecting to mention John's cryptic message about Wayland Smith—which was beginning to look more and more like a legitimate clue instead of a cute come-on meant to lure me into a bargain-package rendezvous with John B. Smythe. It was one hell of a vague clue, though. "Wayland's work" could refer to any one of a hundred objects in a dozen different museums. If John really was planning to steal a historic treasure, and if Leif really was on his trail, Leif presumably knew more about the plot than I did. Besides, that damned message made me sound like a collaborator. I wouldn't have blamed Leif for interpreting it that way. I couldn't figure it out myself.

Why the devil would John warn me of his illegal intentions? He knew I'd do everything possible to thwart him if I took the warning seriously. . . . I hadn't taken it seriously, though. The message had been perfectly framed —vague enough to preclude action on my part, intriguing enough to whet my curiosity. It had done the job. Here I was, right where John wanted me. I wished to God I knew why he wanted me here.

While I pursued this depressing train of thought, Leif watched me intently. After a while he said, "I believe you."

"Thanks a heap. I'd like some dessert, please."

"Certainly." He waved at the waiter and watched benevolently as I consumed something consisting primarily of whipped cream and custard. "I like to see a woman who enjoys her food," he announced.

I glanced at him, licking custard off my upper lip, but he wasn't being funny. "You are right," he went on. "I should not spoil your vacation. I apologize. Let me make amends. I will show you some of the night life of Stockholm."

Things were looking up. I smiled at him. "I'd like that."

There was one minor contretemps, when I hauled my purse out from under the table and checked, as I always do, to make sure the contents were intact. I can never get the darned thing closed—I carry too many things in it— so I was not surprised to find that several items were missing. "My passport," I exclaimed.

Leif eyed the bulging, obscene object critically. "You should keep it always in your hands."

"It's too big." I peered under the table, then shied back as I found myself nose to nose with Leif. His eyeballs gleamed like boiled eggs in the gloom. They looked absolutely disgusting.

"As I thought," he said, fumbling around the floor. "Passport, lipstick, comb . . . What in God's name is this?"

I couldn't tell. It was too dark under the table. We both came up into the light and Leif handed me my belongings, including the object that had prompted his horrified inquiry. I didn't blame him; it must have felt like something long-dead and rotten. I am particularly addicted to a variety of pastry made by a certain bakery in Munich. It's like a jelly doughnut, but squashier. I had forgotten it was in there.

"Sorry," I said, retrieving the collection and putting it in my bag. Leif started to lick his fingers, then thought better of it and wiped them on his napkin. "Is everything there?" he asked, with the doggedly patient look men get when they deal with women's purses.

"I think so. No, wait—my notebook."

We crawled around under the table for a while without success. The waiter watched our activities with poorly concealed alarm; when I explained, he joined the search. Finally he said breathlessly, "Perhaps it has been kicked away, under another table. If you would like me to look . . ."

"There was nothing important in it," I said. "If it turns up, hang on to it. I'll look in next time I'm in the neighborhood."

"Are you sure you don't wish to continue searching?" Leif asked, as we started for the door.

I reassured him. The notebook was new; it contained nothing except a few addresses and miscellaneous notes.

The evening turned out to be a success after all. First we went to a jazz pub—"with jazz," as the advertisement carefully specified. Then we went on to a nightclub and danced. Leif was a marvelous dancer. For so large a man his movements were extraordinarily economical and controlled. Afterward we took a walk along the waterfront. The white boats lifted at anchor and the long lights shimmered across the water. We held hands as we walked, and we didn't talk much. When we finally turned back toward the hotel I had almost forgotten J. Smythe; if I thought of him at all, it was to thank him for inadvertently making it possible for me to meet Leif.

Though the hour was well after midnight, the ground-floor windows of the restaurant and bar were brightly lit, and people streamed in and out of the main doors. Leif escorted me to the desk and waited till I asked for my key. When the clerk handed it over, he also gave me a small sheaf of messages.

"There were several calls, Dr. Bliss. If it is urgent, our switchboard will be open."

Leif had stood to one side like a little gent, pretending not to listen when I mentioned my room number. Curiosity got the better of him when he saw the messages.

"I hope nothing is wrong," he said.

I held the papers up so he could read them. "They're all from Schmidt. Head of the National Museum, as you surely must know."

"Vicky, you do not need to convince me—"

"Just thought I'd mention it."

"He seems to want you very badly."

"I know what he wants. It's not important. Well . . ."

I stuffed the notes in my purse and turned from the desk. Leif bowed stiffly. "Good night, Vicky. Sleep well."

"Oh," I said. "Good night. And thanks."

"May I telephone you tomorrow?"

"Yes, you may."

He bowed again, turned on his heel, and strode away, moving with military precision.

Feigning personal interest is one way of keeping tabs on

a suspect. I preferred to believe he wasn't feigning. He was a gorgeous sight as he made his lordly way through the lesser mortals in the lobby; his flaxen hair clung to his head and covered the nape of his neck like a gilt helmet.

The pleasures of the past few hours had not let me forget certain other matters. I went into my room with all the panache of the Cowardly Lion, an inch at a time, and I didn't relax until after I had searched every corner. No one was there. As far as I could tell, no one had been there.

Four of Schmidt's messages were labeled "Urgent." Before I called him, I had a nice leisurely bath and made myself a cup of coffee with my handy plug-in electric pot. Schmidt is something of a night owl, and besides, I didn't particularly care whether I woke him up. He had his nerve, harassing me when I hadn't even been gone a day.

Naturally I called collect. He wanted to talk; he could pay. He accepted the call without so much as a gulp, and it was then that I began to think I had been mistaken about his reason for calling.

He didn't even say hello. "What are you up to now?" he shrieked. "What is it you think you are doing? A little holiday, you say. The land of your ancestors, you say. You betray me, you lie to me—your friend, your benefactor, your—"

"Wait a minute! I didn't lie to you, Schmidt. Would I do a thing like that?"

"Yes." He stopped to catch his breath. When he resumed he had evidently decided to try subtler tactics. His voice wheedled. "Is it a case like the Riemenschneider, my dear Vicky? Another prize for our museum?"

He was referring to an art object by a medieval German sculptor, which I had located after it had been lost for four hundred years. I had met Schmidt during that bizarre business, and though I would be the first to admit that I had a certain amount of assistance in my quest (none from Schmidt; he was a first-class nuisance from beginning to end), my success had given him an exaggerated idea of my abilities.

"No." I made the negative as convincing as I could. Once Schmidt got a notion in his big round bald head, nothing less than a blunt instrument could get it out. I didn't want him rushing off to Sweden to join in the fun. Where the museum was concerned, he was almost as crooked as John. The two of them together . . . Well, the very idea made cold sweat pop out on my brow.

"I resent your attitude," I went on. "You have no right to make accusations."

Usually Schmidt crumples up when he is attacked. Not this time. "You tell me it is nothing that today I should hear from three persons calling themselves cousins and wishing urgently to find you? Never in all these years has one cousin called. Now it is three in a single day."

"I have about two hundred cousins," I said, after a moment's thought. "We're a prolific family."

"Three? In one day?"

"Did they leave their names?"

"Oh, certainly. One was Cousin Bob."

I have a Cousin Bob. Last I heard he was living in Chicago with his fourth wife and holding down three jobs in order to keep up with his child-support payments. As I said, we are a prolific family. It was barely conceivable that Bob might be in Europe, but it was damned unlikely.

"That's one," I said encouragingly.

"Number two was Cousin George." Schmidt's voice dripped with sarcasm.

I really do have a lot of cousins. I could not recall one named George.

"That's two. Didn't anyone give a last name?"

"Number three did so." Schmidt sounded genuinely puzzled. "He was different from the others, Vicky. He was the first to telephone, and when he said he was the Swedish cousin whom you planned to visit, I thought only that you had missed one another."

A hideous qualm passed through me, surpassing in hideousness all the minor qualms I had felt in the course of the day. I croaked, "I hope to God you didn't tell him where I was staying."

"You take me for an old fool? I told him I could not do that, and he was most gracious. Indeed, he was kind enough to approve. He was glad, he said, that you had so careful and sensible a friend."

"Thanks, Papa Schmidt," I said sincerely.

"Bah," said Schmidt. "He was an old papa too, Vicky. At least his voice sounded like that of an elderly man, and he gave to me not only his name and address but references from everyone except God."

"What?"

"You don't hear me? His name is Gustaf Jonsson." He spelled it. "Was not Johnson your mother's name?"

"My father's mother. How did you know that? You've been snooping in my files again, Schmidt."

"Mr. Gustaf Jonsson told me," Schmidt said stiffly.

I apologized. Schmidt does snoop, sometimes looking for rough drafts of Rosanna's future adventures (little does he know I make them up as I go along), and sometimes out of general inquisitiveness. I don't mind. It keeps him happy.

"Hmph," said Schmidt, when I had abased myself sufficiently. "Have you a pencil? I give you the address and telephone of Mr. Jonsson. He asks that you call him."

I reached for my purse and then remembered my notebook was no longer in it. I wrote the information on the back of one of the messages.

"Okay," I said. "Thanks."

"I hope you have cause to thank me," Schmidt said ominously. "Vicky, I am not happy about this."

I wasn't happy about it either. However, I tried to sound more puzzled than alarmed as I questioned Schmidt about my callers. He couldn't tell me much more. "Bob" and "George" both had ordinary voices, without any accent Schmidt could distinguish. Neither had pressed him for further information after learning that I was out of the country and was not expected back for several weeks. By contrast Mr. Jonsson had been absolutely loquacious. He really had given Schmidt references—two banks and a former minister of state.

"Well, it's all very mysterious," I said. "I appreciate everything you did, Schmidt—and everything you didn't do. I'll be in touch."

I didn't expect to get rid of him that easily, and I didn't. Admonitions, warnings, and suggestions gushed out of him. Finally I hung up.

I got up off the bed where I had been reclining and went to the window. My room was in the front of the hotel, overlooking the quay. I suspected I owed that choice location to Schmidt's influence.

Directly opposite, the "City Between the Bridges" filled its island from shore to shore, its close-packed structures rising in successive tiers. It looked like a single giant building, a citadel or castle, with a thousand lighted windows, and the dark water, streaked with splinters of reflected light, might have been a protective moat.

It was so beautiful I forgot my troubles for a minute and just enjoyed the view. Then I turned my attention to more practical matters, noting with approval that my room was on the fourth (European) floor, and that the nearest balcony was a considerable distance away, below and to the right. The street and the quay in front of the hotel were bright as daylight. Nobody could get at me by way of the window unless he was a human fly. Which John might well be, but being also a cautious man, he would hardly risk crawling up the front of a fully lighted building in plain view of a hundred people.

John was the first person I thought of when Schmidt started listing unknown "cousins." On second thought, however, I doubted that he had been one of them. He wouldn't call himself Bob or George; he'd have given some crazy name like Agrivaine. Also, there was no reason for him to check up on my whereabouts. He knew where I was. He had seen me. No doubt he had also seen the label on my suitcase; he had eyes like a vulture's.

Leif might have been one of the "cousins," checking to make sure that the woman he had seen at the airport carrying Dr. Victoria Bliss's bags was the real Victoria Bliss and not a ringer. But that didn't make sense either. If he was a policeman, he could inquire through official channels without inventing unimaginative names. If he *was* a policeman . . .

I would have liked to believe that Bob and George were John and Leif. The alternative, that several parties unknown and probably inimical were on my trail, was distinctly unpleasant. Most peculiar of all was Cousin Gustaf. Should I get in touch with him? First I thought I would. Then I thought I had better leave well enough alone. Then I decided I would go to bed and let my subconscious wrestle with the dilemma. I have a great deal of faith in my subconscious. Sometimes it's the only part of my brain that works.

Chapter Three

HEN I WOKE UP next morning I felt terrible.
At first I couldn't imagine why. Then I remembered my
cousins. The dilemma was still unresolved. Apparently
my subconscious had taken the night off.

It wasn't until I was brushing my teeth that the dream
came back to me.

Not surprisingly, Leif had been the featured actor.
Dressed in leggings and a tunic open to the waist, his fair
hair shoulder length, he wore a smith's leather apron and
flourished a hammer the size of Thor's fabled Mjolnir.
Outside the crude shelter where he was working was a
sign: "Wayland's Smithy; Good Work at Low Prices. If
you didn't get it at Wayland's, you paid too much."

Hypnotized by the ripple of bronzed muscle on his
arms and chest, I didn't notice the object on the anvil till
his great hammer was high in the air. It wasn't a sword

or a piece of armor, it was a chalice—a footed cup made of silver and bound with strips of gold. Inlaid garnets and scarlet enamel flashed in the light.

My dream self sprang forward with a voiceless shriek, trying to save the precious thing. I was too slow; but just before the hammer struck, a figure materialized out of nowhere and a long, thin arm snatched the chalice away. The figure was that of the silhouette cutter, his face no longer meek and humble, but set in a grin of fiendish triumph. He clutched the chalice to his meager bosom. The hammer crashed on the anvil, starting a progression of ringing vibrations that grew louder and louder. The silhouette cutter began to vibrate, as if the atoms of his body were spinning off into space. His body faded until nothing was left but his grin—and the shape of the chalice, blazing with internal light so dazzling it hurt my eyes.

I decided I needed a cup of coffee. Or three.

While I made it and drank it, I sent a silent apology to my subconscious. It hadn't solved the problem I had set it before I went to bed—to call or not to call Cousin Gustaf—but it had reminded me of something important.

Leif's presence in the dream probably didn't mean anything except that all of my mind, sub- and superconscious, has excellent taste. The silhouette cutter was one of those random contributions one often finds in dreams; he was a bizarre figure, and the encounter had been unusual. The point of the dream was the chalice. It had numerous mythic connotations—Arthurian legend, the Holy Grail, the chalice from the palace. . . . No, that was from an old Danny Kaye movie.

I wrenched my frivolous mind back to business. The important thing was that the dream chalice was no figment of my imagination. It actually existed. I had seen a photograph of it only a few days before.

I had been kidding myself when I tried to dismiss "Wayland's work" as a meaningless joke. The phrase had nagged at me for days, while I packed and shopped and cleaned out the fridge and called the kennel and performed all the other chores my temporary absence required. Finally, the day before I was due to leave, I succumbed. I spent several hours in the museum library, looking up objects to which that enigmatic description might apply.

The reference was even more ambiguous than I had supposed. Wayland was a northern god originally, but his story had traveled far and endured for centuries. "Wayland's work" might describe an art object produced anywhere in northern Europe over a period of several hundred years—Anglo-Saxon, Viking, Celtic—or even treasures brought back from Russia or Byzantium by far-ranging Scandinavian traders.

"That's not my field" is a statement often made by scholars to excuse their ignorance when they are asked to explain something they don't understand. However, northern Europe between 400 and 1100 A.D. is *not* my field. As I browsed in the library that afternoon, going farther and farther from my original research as my interest increased, I realized that, like a good many people, I had underestimated my remote ancestors.

The popular impression of the Germanic tribes is that of bloody-minded savages trampling the delicate blossoms of civilization underfoot. In all the stories I had read they were the villains. The Vikings burned villages, looted churches, raped and murdered; the Saxons fought noble King Arthur and the knights of the Round Table; the Vandals gave their name to successive generations of destroyers. Admittedly they were a crude lot, but their opponents weren't much better. They were courageous explorers, fighters, and traders. The might of Rome, which had crushed the civilized empires of the Near East, faltered and fell in the German forests. Many a Roman standard graced the hut of a Germanic chieftain after the defeat of the legion that had carried it.

The Vikings became the finest seamen of their time, daring the perils of the unknown west. Even I knew that Leif the Lucky had been the first to discover America, centuries before Columbus. What I didn't know, or had forgotten, was that the Scandinavians also followed the caravan routes to the east. The tribes from whom the name "Russia" derives were northerners. Tall blond warriors formed the honor guard of the emperors of Byzantium, and traders brought back coins minted in Damascus, Baghdad, and Tashkent. As a runic inscription on an ancient tombstone put it, "Valiantly we journeyed afar for gold; and in the east we fed the eagles."

Among the objects brought back to Scandinavia by traders or looters was the chalice of my dream. Discovered by a farmer plowing his field, it had been buried over a thousand years earlier by an owner fearing attack on his home. He had never retrieved it. Perhaps the powdery traces of his bones had been scattered by the same plow that turned up his treasure.

The chalice was now in a private collection in Stockholm, which undoubtedly explained its appearance in my dream. The name and address of the museum was in my lost notebook, along with other notes I had taken that afternoon. The loss was not irretrievable; I could find the same reference books in local institutions. Or I could call Gerda, Schmidt's secretary, and ask her to look up the information.

The hell with it, I thought. And the hell with Cousin Gustaf, too. No busman's holidays for me.

I hung around the room for another hour, fighting off energetic chambermaids who wanted to clean, and hoping the telephone would ring. I used all the makeup I normally don't have time to bother with, and tried on three different outfits before I settled on white slacks and T-shirt, with a kelly green scarf. I did my nails. The phone still didn't ring, so I cleaned out my purse. Among the papers in it was the slip of paper on which I had scribbled Cousin Gustaf's address. Schmidt had also given me the references Gustaf had mentioned. Odd, that; it was the sort of thing John might do, inventing unnecessary and seemingly respectable references to disarm suspicion. One of the banks was in Stockholm. I toyed with the idea of calling, but my resentment against all the known and unknown characters who were trying to louse up my vacation was too strong. I put the papers back in my purse. The phone did not ring. I threw away the jelly doughnut. The phone did not ring.

At eleven o'clock I admitted the maid. The hell with Leif too. I would dedicate the day to sightseeing and shopping of the most frivolous kind. No museums, no antiquities. Maybe I could pick up another tall blond. There were plenty of them in Sweden.

Stockholm, which is often cool and rainy, put on one of her better shows for me that day. The colors were those of springtime innocence—clear greens, sparkling blues, soft red brick, and creamy buff. The breeze was just cool enough to justify my decision to look for a hand-knit ski sweater.

I moved out of the way of the stream of traffic, pedestrian and vehicular, that passed the doors of the Grand Hotel, and consulted my pocket map of Stockholm. Up Kungsträdgårdsgatan, along the park, to Hamngatan; wriggle through a small square and a side street to Drottninggatan, "long, narrow and filled with tiny shops," according to the guidebook.

Presumably I followed that route, and obviously I did not get hit by a taxi, but I don't remember a thing about it. The shop windows finally roused me from my reveries. Clothes and food (and a couple of other things) appeal to basic instincts even more compelling than the worries that continued to nag at my mind. I tried on fifteen or sixteen sweaters, each more gorgeous than the last. The one I bought was a blend of green and gray and red and black, with silver clasps; and after I had paid for it I decided I had better start thinking seriously about finding a cheaper hotel. Prices were lower than in Munich, but not much.

By that time it was after one-thirty, so I went to satisfy another basic urge. (I am referring to food.) One of the restaurants fronting Kungsträdgården, formerly the royal gardens, would be just the ticket. I would sit on the terrace in my new red-and-green sweater and drink beer and eat smorgasbord and look at the flowers and watch the children play.

All those amenities were available. In the cooler northern climate the flowers that had come and gone in Munich were still blooming their heads off. The lilacs filled the air with scent, and neatly cultivated beds of freesia and roses made patches of color between the paths where the children ran. But as I sat there poking at my food, I finally came to grips with my problem. That morning I had seen—actually seen and noticed—thirty ski sweaters and two thousand faces. Instead of admiring handsome modern streets and quaint markets, I had been searching for a well-known profile.

Not Leif's. John haunted me like the ghost of an old murder. I hadn't seen him for over twenty-four hours.

Instead of reassuring me, that fact only made me exceedingly nervous.

His inadequate disguise at the airport might have been a precaution against me. He couldn't be sure I would not be followed off the plane by half a dozen Munich cops. (I was sorry now I hadn't thought of it.) However, by the time I reached the currency exchange, he had had me under surveillance for some time, and he must have been reasonably certain I was alone. My jovial hail wouldn't have sent him scuttling for cover if I were the only person he had to worry about. My first assumption had been correct after all. Somebody was on his trail.

I had expected to hear from him before this. I had left the hotel that morning and walked, aimlessly and slowly, hoping he would seize the opportunity to contact me.

Men *had* tried to contact me. Two student types, a little Japanese gent draped with cameras, and a well-dressed, sanctimonious-looking man whose nationality was obscure, but whose command of English included some surprising words. None had been John. If he was following me, he was doing it very skillfully. If someone else was following me, he or she was also doing it very skillfully. In the bloom of my carefree youth I used to think I was a match for any number of villains, but I was older and wiser now, and I had to admit I probably wouldn't spot a specific pursuer unless he was bright blue or wore a clown costume. People are so annoyingly conformist. All middle-aged, middle-sized businessmen dress alike, and students are the most conservative of all; most of the males were sporting beards that summer, and ninety percent of them, male and female, wore designer jeans and T-shirts. A couple at a table nearby resembled most of the young people I had seen that morning: dark glasses cov-

ered the upper halves of their faces, and her close-cropped
brown hair and his whiskers were part of the informal
uniform they all slavishly followed.

My eyes moved over the other diners. The only thing
I could be sure of was that Leif wasn't among them. His
height made him as conspicuous as a clown or a painted
Pict. Whatever disguise he might adopt, he couldn't hide
that.

Then my roving eye focused on something that was
familiar—a shabby gray sweater and a massive head of
gray hair. His shoulders had an obsequious stoop as he
addressed a group of older women sitting at a table for six.
The women were laughing and shaking their heads.

As if he felt my eyes upon him, the little man straightened and turned. Across the width of the room our
glances locked. He bowed and smiled. Balancing his briefcase awkwardly on one arm, he opened it and reached
inside. The card he held up, like a picket's poster, was
only too familiar. There I was, in featureless outline, for
all the restaurant to see.

I couldn't be angry; he was so eager and so proud of his
work, and so obviously in need of assistance in selling his
unusual product. When he gestured at me, at the silhouette, and at the ladies, I nodded, embarrassed but unable
to resist the appeal. With an even deeper bow he turned
back to the women to make his pitch. They had the unmistakable stamp of happy American widows taking their
annual summer holiday. I had seen a number of such
parties in Munich. They clung to the bouffant hairdos of
twenty years ago, and they always wore nice knit pant-
suits. Now they were peering at me through their bifocals,
nodding and laughing as the silhouette cutter demonstrated his skill with me as the model.

I felt like one of those antique advertising posters that

have two big hands with pointing fingers indicating the object of interest. One of the ladies waved at me. With a shrug I waved back. The silhouette cutter sat down and took out his materials. He had made his sale.

The brief interlude had distracted and entertained me, but as soon as it was over, I started worrying at the old problem again like a dog with a used bone. Only a few hours earlier I had determined to ignore all the intriguing little clues that led into trails of meaningless conjecture and possible disaster. It would be my own fault if I followed one of those trails. Nobody was bothering me. Yet, knowing John, I couldn't believe I was in the clear. He wouldn't drag me all the way up here and abandon . . . not me, he'd do that in a second . . . abandon the purpose for which he had summoned me. Even his apparent inaction had meaning, and my own inaction might be leaving me wide open to his next ploy.

Naturally I had thought of the most obvious reason for his failure to get in touch with me. The people who had been chasing him might have caught up with him. If they were police, he could be in jail. If they weren't . . .

I imagined myself calling the Stockholm morgue. "Got any surplus bodies today? A man about thirty-five, five eleven and a half, slight, fair-haired—or maybe black, or gray, or bald . . ."

There was bound to be someone of that description lying around. Any large city has its share of murders and suicides and accidents. The extensive stretches of water in Stockholm must be a temptation to despairing lovers, drunken tourists, and exasperated spouses.

I didn't really believe he was dead. No, he was skulking around somewhere, plotting and planning in a Machiavellian fashion.

I finished my beer and summoned the waiter. As I fumbled for the money to pay the check, I felt a surge of well-being. Indecision is the one thing that drives me crazy. Probably the decision I had reached was the wrong one, but it was better than doing nothing.

On my way out I passed the table where the man in gray was at work. Two of the ladies were giggling over their portraits, and he was engaged on number three. Seeing me, the chubbiest of the girls (I'm sure that's how they referred to themselves) gave me a dimpled grin and held up her silhouette. It was a masterpiece, subtly flattering, and even more subtly caricaturing her worst features—multiple chins, pinched mouth, receding forehead. I did not pause to admire it, I just smiled and nodded and went on. The ladies smiled and nodded. People at nearby tables smiled and nodded. The silhouette cutter smiled and nodded. . . . And I'm sure any astute reader of thrillers has surely, by this time, caught the implications I flat-out missed. Take the "had I but known" comment as read.

Innocent and stupid and unaware, I ambled into the park and paused to consult my map. Strandvägen, the wide boulevard along the waterfront, looked like the most direct route. And I had better hurry. Museums keep peculiar hours; some are open in the evening, some close at four o'clock.

The long white boats glided over the water, carrying carefree tourists on their way. I wished I were one of them. I wasn't even sure why I was heading for the Statens Historiska Museum. I wanted to refresh my memories of Viking art objects and take some notes to replace the ones in my lost notebook, but my real reason was far less sensible. The dream kept itching at my mind. I could account rationally for almost all the elements of it, including the anxiety that had led me to visualize a masterpiece threatened with destruction. Any art object John was after had a poor chance of survival; it would probably vanish into the limbo of lost treasures. But I couldn't explain the chalice itseif. Why that, of all the other examples in museums—the Kingston brooch, the golden horns from Gallehus? I wanted a closer look at that chalice, and I needed the address of the private museum that owned it. Someone at the National Museum of Antiquities would be able to supply that information.

I was only a block or two from the museum when I saw a stationer's and went in to get a replacement for my notebook. It was then that, with the abruptness of pure illogic, I remembered the name of the place I was looking for.

The clerk was very helpful. He looked up the name and address and showed me where it was on the map. As I might have expected, I had gone in the wrong direction. The Hansson Collection was on Riddarholm Island on the far side of Gamla Stan.

Every large city has places like the Hansson Collection—small, privately endowed museums that are dedicated to a particular specialty and are visited only by experts in that specialty and by compulsive tourists who follow lists of "things to see." The building in which it was housed had once been a private residence—that of Mr. Hansson, I assumed. It was a beautiful seventeenth-century mansion in the ornate Dutch Renaissance style, with rosy-red bricks and carved window frames. I lucked out on the schedule. It was open from one to five. I still had an hour.

I passed through room after stately room, my footsteps echoing, in spite of my efforts to tread lightly. The focus of the place was prehistory. I don't think I saw more than six people, all of them frozen in rapt contemplation of shapeless stone axes and rotted copper tools. Prehistory is definitely not my field, and I have never had any trouble resisting exhibits of cracked pots, but I must confess to a certain morbid interest in graves. A goodly proportion of the objects displayed in archeological museums come from tombs, but that isn't the reason why reconstructions of ancient burials are so popular with visitors. I suppose they remind us of the futility of material ambitions and the inevitability of death. "As I am now, so you shall be. . . ."

Since I didn't need reminders of mortality just then, I headed directly for the Treasure Room, where the most valuable pieces in the collection were housed—valuable, at least, in material terms. The arrangement had been made not so much for the convenience of tourists as for security. Like our treasure room in Munich, it was built like a vault, windowless and steel-walled.

Reaching the end of the wing, I turned a corner and came to a sudden, shocked halt. I'm sure the exhibit has been deliberately arranged to have that effect. Sensitive tourists of either sex probably shrieked.

She lay on her back, her head turned to one side and her limbs lightly flexed in an attitude of sleep. The brown ribs showed through the flattened chest wall, and one hand modestly covered the sexual area, but there was no doubt she was female; the rounded hips and slender arms had been petrified into a variety of tanned leather. Her head had been shaved. The delicate folds of her ear had been flattened by the earth that held her down, and a strip of woven cloth covered her eyes. They had at least had the decency to blindfold her before they drowned her in the bog and left her there.

I had read about the bodies found in peat bogs, incredibly preserved by natural chemicals. They aren't mummies, for mummification implies a drying process. This is more like tanning. Some of the bog people, like the man from Tollund, are more lifelike than most Egyptian mummies. The majority of them come from Denmark. This girl—fourteen years old, according to the catalog—had been found in Halland, on the west coast of Sweden. She had died sometime during the first century A.D., a sacrifice to some unknown god, or an executed criminal. It was hard to think of a crime a fourteen-year-old would commit. The catalog suggested adultery. Fourteen years old . . . Many of the women were married that young. And throughout the centuries, up to modern times, women convicted of adultery often had their hair cut off before they were killed. Only the women. Their male partners in "crime" probably handed the barber his razors and then headed for the local pub to drink a few horns of mead with the boys.

As I went on into the next room, I heard a muffled shriek, as another unwary visitor came on the girl from Halland.

There were two people in the Treasure Room. One looked like a student—beard, jeans, T-shirt. He was leaning over a glass case containing coins and beads.

The other person was a woman, and for a startled second I felt as if I had come upon my doppelgänger, that image of oneself that is the harbinger of imminent death. Like me, she was unusually tall; like me, she had long blond hair. Like me, she wore white slacks. There the resemblance stopped. Her blouse had long, full sleeves and an unnecessary profusion of ruffles around the neck and shoulders. Compared to her mane of shimmering hair, mine was lank and lustreless—like the before and after in a shampoo commercial. Her hips were as straight as a boy's, but any deficiency in that area was compensated for up above. She must have been wearing a bra. Nobody's muscles are that good.

The chalice was in a separate case in the middle of the room. My dreaming mind had an excellent visual memory; it had reproduced the major features. The shallow bowl and the wide foot were joined by a band of heavy gold overlaid with exquisitely coiled filigree. A band of the same material encircled the bowl just below the rim. This band and the twin handles were inlaid with garnets and scarlet enamel, set off by the gold strips of the cloisons in which the enamel was set. The intricacy of the design was incredible. It was hard to imagine how it could have been done without a magnifying glass. Two of these relatively modern devices had been set up inside the case in order to enlarge portions of the filigree.

Color photography is superb these days, but nothing can capture the true wonder of work like that. You have to see it. As I bent over the lovely thing, I heard the bearded man walk out. The woman was moving methodically around the room, stopping at every exhibit.

The catalog contained a long paragraph on the chalice. Discovered in 1889, one of the first objects presented by Karl Hansson when he contributed his collection to the city.

Footsteps moved toward me. Without looking up from the catalog I stepped to one side to give the newcomer a better view. It was her perfume that caught my attention —divine. I couldn't identify it, probably because it smelled like money as well as musk, the kind of money I've never possessed.

Golden locks tumbled over her face as she bent to look more closely at the chalice. I caught only a glimpse of a tanned cheek, but that was all I needed. He heard my breath catch, and that was all *he* needed. Before I could express myself with the eloquence the situation demanded, he said in a hideous falsetto, "Aren't you the clever little thing! I felt sure you would figure it out."

I ejected one word—"You—" before he cut off the noun. "I beg, dear girl, that you won't shout. I believe I've lost him, but one can never take too many precautions."

"Who is 'him'?" I inquired. I spoke softly. I didn't want to attract "his" attention either.

A less subtle comedian might have made some stupid joke about grammar. John just brushed the voluminous hair back from his face and grinned. I understood the necessity for the fluffy blouse; he was no weight lifter, but his biceps could never have passed for a woman's, and his shoulders were broad enough to require camouflage. And, as I studied his pensive profile, I also understood the dark makeup.

"I see you've already had a little set-to with him," I said.

Wincingly John touched the bruise on his jaw. There were others around his throat, almost hidden by the ruffles.

"You needn't sound so pleased. He caught me off guard. It won't happen again."

"I'll bet. Who is 'him'?"

"No one you'd care to meet, and no one you need worry about. It's a private matter. Nothing to do with the present—er—"

"Swindle," I suggested.

"Matter. Affair?" He turned an inquiring, amused blue eye in my direction.

"You're not my type," I said. "Particularly not in that outfit. How you'd have the gall to think I'd fall for your machinations again, after—"

"Keep your voice down. I admit I owe you an explanation about Paris—"

"And a lot of other things."

"And a lot of other things. But this isn't the time or the place. Though I'm ninety-nine percent certain that my friend doesn't want to kill anyone except me—"

"There is that one percent," I said apprehensively.

"There is. And where you are concerned, my heart's dearest, those odds are too high. I'll drop in this evening, around midnight. Three knocks, then a pause, then two knocks."

I started to say something sarcastic, but he looked so ridiculous pawing at his hair, with those preposterous breasts jutting out at an impossible angle as he bent over the case, that my sense of humor got the better of me. I didn't want him to see me laugh, so I turned and sat down on one of the velvet-covered couches surrounding the pièce de résistance, the case containing the chalice.

"What are you going to look like next time I see you?" I asked.

John sat down beside me. "Not like this. I've already shaved twice today, and my skin is quite sensitive."

"You make a very pretty girl."

"I knew you were going to say that. What's your room number?"

"First tell me what this friend of yours looks like."

Half a lifetime of eluding the law had made John quick at catching undertones. He turned so abruptly that I jumped. My purse slid off my lap and spilled half its contents onto the floor.

"Have you acquired a friend too?" he asked intently.

"I may have."

"Medium height, heavy-set, brown hair and beard, horn-rimmed glasses?"

"No."

"Sure? He could have shaved the beard—"

"No chance. Mine is blond, seven feet tall."

"Hmmm. Do I perchance scent a rival?"

"Definitely. Speaking of scent, what is that perfume?"

"Like it?" John turned a ruffled shoulder to me and batted his eyelashes. They weren't false. His eyelashes are one of his best features, and he knows it.

"Love it."

"Then I know what to get you for your birthday. Gather up your gear and get lost, darling. I'll see you tonight."

"But I want to know—"

"Later." He began picking up my scattered possessions. Instead of kneeling, he moved in a shuffling squat—afraid to dirty the knees of his white slacks, I suppose. I was about to join the pursuit when all of a sudden he went absolutely rigid. His knees hit the floor. Stiff as a marble statue of a supplicant he knelt, staring at the papers he held.

During the course of our Roman adventure I had seen John face assorted perils—guns, dogs, maniacal killers—with relative aplomb. His appearance of Best British sangfroid was not due to courage but to his insane sense of humor; he couldn't resist making smart remarks even when the subject of his ridicule was brandishing a knife under his nose. When the wisecracks gave out, he reverted to type, groaning over every little scratch and trying to hide behind any object in the neighborhood, including my skirts. I'd seen him turn pale green with fright and livid with terror. I had never seen him look the way he looked now.

I let out a muffled croak. John leaped up as if he had knelt on a scorpion. Thrusting the papers into my lap, he reached the doorway in three long leaps and disappeared.

There were three papers in the lot he had handed me. One was the message from Schmidt, on the back of which

I had scribbled Gustaf Jonsson's home address. One was a receipt from the store where I had bought my sweater. The last was my silhouette.

I put them in my purse. I was looking around to make sure John hadn't missed something when I heard a harsh cough. Someone was coming. Slow, shuffling footsteps, heavy asthmatic breathing. . . .

The man who appeared in the doorway wore a uniform like that of a guard. That's what he was—a museum guard. He glanced incuriously at me and walked slowly around the room inspecting the cases.

He was the only person I saw on the way out. The museum was about to close. Everyone else had gone. No seven-foot-tall Vikings, no short, bearded men with horn-rimmed glasses, no overdeveloped females wearing flaxen wigs. I ought to have been relieved. I felt squirmy all over, as if hundreds of eyes were watching me.

After I had walked a few blocks in the bright summer sunlight the feeling dissipated. Maybe John's wide-eyed horror had been one of his peculiar jokes, a gimmick designed to allow him to get away before I could ask any more questions.

The most interesting question of all was the one I had failed to pick up on because I was distracted by his disguise. He had been there before me. He might have followed me and reached the treasure room by another route. But his first words had been a compliment on my astuteness. "I felt sure you would figure it out." Figure what out? Had he known I would find my way to the Hansson collection? The chalice did mean something.

I found a café and ordered coffee. Taking the catalog of the Hansson collection from my purse, I turned to the description of the chalice.

The answer jumped out of the surrounding print as if

it were outlined in red—one word that linked the jumbled fragments together into a coherent whole. The name of the chalice.

Yes, it had a name. Many unique objects do—the Ardagh chalice, the Kingston brooch, the Sutton Hoo treasure. They are called after the places where they were found, in tombs and barrows and fields. The proper name of my treasure was the Karlsholm chalice.

My eyes had passed over that word a dozen times without noting its significance, but my good old reliable subconscious had made the connection—that inward eye that is the bliss of solitude and, upon occasion, the salvation of Bliss. Wordsworth's inward eye had turned up daffodils. Mine had produced the chalice itself, without outré symbolism or Freudian nonsense. And I had missed it again. This time I couldn't miss it. Only moments earlier I had glanced at the paper with Gustaf's address. That's where he lived—in Karlsholm.

Chapter Four

I DECIDED to go back to the hotel instead of struggling with the intricacies of a pay phone. I found several messages waiting for me. Two were from Schmidt, one was from Leif. The latter had called at eleven-ten, right after I left the hotel. He had not left a number, but said he would call back at six.

I looked at my watch. It was already after five, too late for some of the calls I needed to make. Served me right, too. I should have taken action that morning instead of trying to play ostrich. Nasty things don't go away when you hide your head, that just gives them a chance to sneak up on you.

I tried the bank first, on the off chance, but there was no answer. Bankers' hours are the same everywhere. Next I called Schmidt. His messages were always marked "Urgent," but in view of the revelations of the previous evening I thought I had better take these "Urgents" seriously. Schmidt kept erratic hours—being the director, he could keep any hours he liked—and, having neither kith nor kin, wife nor child, he often stayed late at the office.

I almost dropped the phone when I heard the voice of Schmidt's secretary. Gerda's punctual departures are a staff joke; it is claimed that the wind of her passage out of the office can knock a strong man flat. I said, "What did you do, sit on a tube of glue?"

Gerda was not amused. She said stiffly, "Herr Professor Dr. Director Schmidt has departed. He asked me to remain to deliver a message."

"To me?"

"Aber natürlich," Gerda said. It is also a staff joke that I am Schmidt's pet. I'm not supposed to know that, but of course I do.

"That was kind of you," I said, in my most ingratiating voice. "What's the message?"

Gerda switched to English. Her self-conscious voice and stumbling pronunciation showed she was reading aloud.

" 'Cousin Gustaf checks out with carillon. Golden boys say he is night attire of felines, Empress of Germany.' "

After a moment I said, "You had better give me that again."

She gave it to me again. I scribbled. Then I said, "I appreciate it, Gerda. Thanks a lot. You run on home. Oh—were there any calls for me today?"

"Nein."

"Gerda, are you mad at me?"

"Nein."

"Then why do you sound like the Ice Queen?"

"Herr Director Schmidt has said, 'Read the message, then shut up.' " The phrase she used was German slang, not exactly vulgar, but definitely not the kind of language she was accustomed to hearing from Schmidt, who treated women with the courtliness of a vanished age.

I thought it over. Then I said cunningly, "If he had not said that, is there anything you would tell me?"

Gerda giggled. *"Nein,"* she said.

I tried a few more subtle tricks and got a few more *nein*'s. It was unlikely that Schmidt would confide in her; he hadn't a high opinion of her intelligence or discretion.

So I bade her good-night and turned to Schmidt's message. It was mystification for the fun of it, serving no useful purpose. Gerda wouldn't understand outdated American slang, but there was no earthly reason why he had to give it to her in code.

All it said was that Cousin Gustaf was in the clear. With bells on. Schmidt had called the bank references (damn his nosy, interfering ways) and had been told that Mr. Jonsson was the cat's pajamas—or words to that effect. I had heard the phrase, probably from my grandmother, and knew it implied approbation. The final comment confirmed that meaning. The Empress of Germany was the Kaiser's wife, and as we all know, Caesar's wife is above reproach. Which was more than I could say for Schmidt's literary style.

The information was reassuring, and it fit the theory I had begun to construct. Even so, I crossed my fingers and took a deep breath before I made the next call.

Did you ever fall in love with a voice? I don't mean the voice of a singer, like Elvis or Lennon or Luciano Pavarotti. Just an ordinary speaking voice, saying ordinary words: "Hello. This is Gustaf Jonsson."

I assumed that was what he said. He spoke Swedish. It's hard to describe the quality of his voice. It was deep and gentle and calm, with a remarkable timbre, like a clear humming. It sounded like my father, though it didn't resemble Dad's gruff, grumbly tones. It sounded like everybody's father. Oh, hell, I can't describe it; all I can say is that the moment he spoke I forgot any lingering suspicions of Gustaf Jonsson.

"Mr. Jonsson?" I stammered. "Hi. Hello, there. This is Vicky. Victoria Bliss."

"Victoria!" He didn't raise his voice, but it sang with delight. "I am so glad! You are so good to telephone me. You are well? You are not ill or injured?"

"No, I'm fine. I—er—" I couldn't ask Everybody's Dad the questions I had intended to ask. "Who the hell are you, Mr. Jonsson? Where did you get the crazy idea I was your cousin?"

"There was some confusion," I said finally. "I—uh—I changed hotels. . . ."

"Yes, I am so glad. The Grand is a good hotel."

"How did you know I was staying at the Grand?"

He hesitated, then said even more softly, "I apologize to you. When I found you were not at the Excelsior, I inquired of several other hotels. I feared there had been an accident."

"You knew I was here, but you didn't call me?"

"It would have been to intrude," Gustaf said simply. "Your Aunt Ingeborg said you desired to visit me, but a young lady does not always desire what her aged aunt believes she desires. I am aged too, and dull. I understand if you do not wish to waste time with me."

I had hoped that if he talked long enough, he would give me the information I needed without my having to dig for it, but this speech turned my brain numb. I felt like a computer feeding back what someone has put into it. I said feebly, "Aunt—Aunt Ingeborg?"

"Yes; it was so good of her to write to me. She found

me through a genealogist, when tracing the history of your family. Genealogy is my hobby too—quite a coincidence, would you not say? Always I meant to investigate the American branch. It must stem, I believe, from Great-great-uncle Johann, who ran away from home at the young age of fifteen and was not heard of again. His grieving mother believed he had drowned, but I always wondered . . ." He broke off, with a grandfatherly chuckle. "You see how it is? When I speak of my hobby I forget good manners. As I wrote to Miss Ingeborg, it would make me so very glad to see you. I do not entertain—I am a grouchy old recluse, in fact—"

"Then perhaps I shouldn't intrude."

"No, no, I say it badly, I am so stupid. I mean only to warn you that you may be bored. But you are not a stranger, you are kin. For those of the same blood my door is always open."

"I'd love to come."

"You are sure? I do not force you?"

"You'd have to use force to keep me away," I said grimly.

"I am so glad! Tomorrow, is it too soon? I am so glad! I will send my car. It is only a five, perhaps six, hours' drive. Will nine o'clock in the morning be too early?"

The bank references should have warned me that Cousin Gustaf was the kind of man who sent cars to pick up unknown relatives. "Nine o'clock?" I repeated stupidly.

"It is too early?"

It definitely was too early—not only for me, but for the unfortunate chauffeur who would have to get up at three A.M. As I hesitated, Gustaf went on, "Ten o'clock? Eleven o'clock? Twelve—"

"Twelve o'clock would be fine."

"I am so glad. You will know the car. . . . No, best I should give Tomas a letter. You will read it before you get in the car, then you will know he is the right person. That is the proper way to do it. You will be safe with Tomas. He is a married man, very dependable, very honest."

I assured him that I was not at all worried about being sold into white slavery by Tomas, though not in those precise words, and hung up with his reiterated expressions of gladness ringing in my ears.

Talking to Cousin Gustaf had been quite an experience. I felt so undone that I collapsed across the bed. So he had heard from Aunt Ingeborg. He must have employed a good medium. Aunt Ingeborg had died the previous October.

The main outlines of the plot were fairly clear now. If my surmises were correct, and I felt sure they were, it was absolutely imperative that I visit Gustaf Jonsson. That sweet, kindly old man had to be warned.

I was still prone, picturing medieval torture devices with a certain smirking Englishman as the central feature, when the phone rang. I glanced at my watch. Six o'clock, on the dot.

"Where have you been all the day?" he demanded.

" 'Henry, my son,' " I said.

"What?"

"Sorry, I wasn't thinking."

"What?"

"Are you sure you don't know where I went today?"

"How could I know? When I telephoned you had left the hotel. I believed we were to meet for lunch."

"You should have shared your belief with me."

"What?"

"What do you want, Leif?"

"To take you to dinner," said Leif.

"You just want to pump me about Smythe."

"You have seen him?"

"No," I said flatly.

"Oh. Anyway, I will take you to dinner."

"Thanks."

"I will come at six-thirty."

"You will come at seven. I'll be downstairs."

I went down at twenty to seven and settled in a quiet corner of the lobby near the bar, where I could keep an eye on the door. Before Leif arrived I had turned down two pressing invitations to have a drink. Neither came from a middle-sized man wearing horn-rimmed glasses. I saw several people who fit that general description; it made me realize how vague it was.

At precisely seven o'clock Leif came through the door. The suit he had worn the previous day had been a cheap ready-made, and rather too small; I suppose he'd have trouble finding something that fit even in a shop that catered to "tall, large men." That evening he featured wrinkled cotton khaki pants and a short-sleeved knit shirt that had seen better days. I deduced that we were dining informally.

If I hadn't known better, I would have sworn he was glad to see me—me myself, not a potential informer. A smile replaced his abstracted frown when he saw me and his eyes moved from my face to my feet and back again with the proper degree of appreciation. As I was beginning to preen myself, he said, "No word from Smythe?"

"You might at least pretend you're interested," I said.

"In you? I am, of course. If I cared only about Smythe, I would seek information by telephone instead of taking you to dinner."

He offered a stiff bent elbow. Stifling a smile, I took it. On the whole I was more inclined to believe Leif's blunt comments than the florid endearments of certain other people.

I suggested we go back to the same restaurant so I could ask about my notebook, but Leif was firm. He had another place in mind. It was a pretty café, with tables on a balcony overlooking some stretch of water or other, but the prices on the menu were considerably lower than those of the other restaurant. Studying it, I muttered, " 'Why is it no one ever sent me yet, One perfect limousine, do you suppose?' "

Predictably, Leif said, "What?"

"Nothing." I wondered whether this evening's outing would go on his expense account. The prices didn't prove anything one way or the other. The only people I know who enjoy lavish expense accounts are politicians and business executives.

Covertly I studied my companion over the top of my menu. He wasn't looking at me. One finger nervously stroked his mustache; the other hand beat a restless tattoo on the table as his eyes moved around the room, inspecting the faces of the diners. I had been too preoccupied with my own thoughts to notice that he had something on his mind too. He was looking for someone—possibly John, possibly someone else. But if he was a policeman of any variety, I was a Short Person.

He just didn't have the right look. I'm not referring to his physical appearance; as we all know from movies and television, undercover cops aren't supposed to look like cops; they are supposed to look like pushers or hookers or crooks. But all of them have one thing in common—professionalism. They wouldn't live long if they didn't know their trade. Leif's performance as a member of the Special Branch had a few glaring flaws. The way he picked me up, for instance—pretty crude, for a pro. Yet he knew me, my reputation and my background, including the fact that I was on good terms with members of the Munich police. So why didn't he take me into his confidence if he wanted me to help him? And if he didn't want my help, why was he hanging around?

There was an obvious answer to that question, but I wasn't conceited enough to believe it. He was mildly interested, but it was only too apparent that he was even more interested in John. Surely he didn't suspect me of being John's confederate. Even if he knew about the Paris affair. . . . If he was a police official, he probably did know about it; the whole damned embarrassing business was on record at the Sûreté. However, the French police had cleared me completely, and if Leif was familiar with that episode he would have every reason to assume I wanted to get even with John. There was only one thing I could think of that might arouse official suspicions of my present trip, and that was the message John had sent. I had flushed it down the toilet in a fit of pique—but the package had been opened before I received it.

Maybe Leif was a cop after all. It isn't easy for a private citizen to interfere with the mails.

I decided it was time to get a few things off my chest. "You owe me an explanation," I said.

Leif started. "What?"

"You heard me. All you've told me is that you are following John Smythe. . . . No, damn it, you haven't even told me that much. Were you following him? Is that why you were at the airport—or were you waiting for me to show up? Why didn't you arrest him when I identified him? Do you suspect me? Was one of your men following me today, and is six to midnight your shift?"

I had Leif's complete attention now. He quit fiddling with his mustache and folded his hands on the table. He was trying to look cool, but the whitened grip of his fingers destroyed the image.

"It is known that you have been in communication with Smythe," he said.

"How? Mind you, I'm not admitting that I have; I'm just asking what gives you that idea."

"I am not at liberty to divulge my sources. You understand—"

"No, I don't understand. I'm sick and tired of oblique hints and vague accusations. And, what's more—"

"Be quiet!"

My rising voice had attracted attention. Fortunately for me, he had stopped me before my big flapping mouth had made any damaging admissions or accusations.

We glared at one another. Leif was breathing so hard the air from his nostrils made the ends of his mustache flap. After a moment his tight lips relaxed and he chuckled softly.

"The little kitten spits and hisses," he said. "It is charming. I suppose many men have told you that you are beautiful when you are angry."

"No," I said. "You're the first."

He looked pleased. I guess he thought I was complimenting him. "Have you any more questions, little lady?" he asked.

"Suppose you answer the ones I've already asked."

"Certainly. But not here. We will walk, and find a place where we can talk privately."

When we left the café he took my hand and continued to hold it as we strolled along the quay. The sun was setting; it would go on setting for hours, hanging around like an unwanted guest. The water reflected the deepening blue of the western sky. The tall masts of the sailing ship *Wasa,* now a youth hostel, lifted like pointing fingers.

She was a beautiful craft, long and sleek. I decided that if Leif suggested a boat ride, I would make damned good and sure the boat was crowded. Yet it was difficult for me to be afraid of a man who called me little lady and told me I was beautiful when I was angry. I couldn't imagine a cop using a tired old line like that one—in fact, I couldn't imagine any man under seventy using it. Was he, or was he not?

He didn't suggest a boat ride. He didn't say anything until we reached Kungsträdgården. Then he announced, "This will be suitable," and looked around for an empty bench.

There weren't many. People were watching a chess game, played on a giant board laid out on the pavement, with wooden men several feet high. Children were at play; couples were talking and drinking and making out. Watching one such pair, intriguingly entwined, Leif shook his head disapprovingly. "Such people."

" 'They are the dirtiest of creatures,' " I said. " 'And they do not wash themselves after sex.' "

"What?"

" 'Furthermore, women have the right to claim a divorce. They do this whenever they wish.' "

"What?"

"Ibn-Fal-Ibrahim al-Tartushi said that in the tenth century, when he visited Scandinavia."

"I do not understand what you are talking about."

"Everything is relative. *Autre temps, autre mœurs.*"

"We will sit here," Leif said, abandoning hope of making sense out of my comments.

The bench he selected was in a quiet corner under a clump of lilacs. We sat down. Leif put his arm around me and mashed me against his side.

"Now we appear like innocent lovers," he explained.

"Uh-huh." There were plenty of people around. Two nearby benches were occupied, and pedestrians passed constantly. "Now, then," I said.

"Always business first, eh?" Leif chuckled and squeezed me. My breath came out in a grunt.

"I am sorry; I forget my strength," Leif said, relaxing his grip a trifle.

"Leif, you're stalling."

"No, no, I don't stall. Believe, Vicky, I have full trust in you. In your honor, at least. But you are too trusting. What are your feelings for that evil man?"

"John?" I hadn't thought of him as evil. Tricky, dishonest, sneaky . . . "I hate the bastard," I said.

"I am glad you don't love him," Leif said. "He is not the man for you, my Valkyrie. He is too small."

I wanted to laugh, but couldn't because Leif had given me another hug and I was short of breath. When I got it back, I said, "Were you following John or waiting for me? Why didn't you arrest him at the airport?"

Leif's right hand began making little sorties, hither and yon. The sweater frustrated him at first, but he dealt with it rather ingeniously. "I did not arrest him because we must catch him in the act. We have no proof, only suspicions."

"Suspicions of what?"

Leif's left hand, hitherto unoccupied, came swooping around like a cable car on a wire. When the heel of his hand was under my chin, his fingers curled up over the crown of my head. He turned my face toward his. His pupils looked like big chunks of amber. His mustache tickled my nose. My lips parted. I was about to sneeze. He muffled the explosion with a kiss. When he let me go I tasted blood. (That's not a complaint, it's only a comment.)

"You distract me," he said gravely.

"I distract *you?*"

"Yes. Have you more questions?"

I will not claim that I had not enjoyed that kiss. It was a masterful performance. I was pretty sure now that Leif was not what he pretended to be and, what is more, I resented his attempt to distract my feeble feminine brain by making love to me. However, his hand was resting on the back of my neck, and I despise characters who blurt out their suspicions to the villain. "Then it was you who destroyed Sir Reginald's suicide note! But that—that means . . ." "Yes, my dear, you have stumbled on the essential clue. Now I am forced to silence you before you can tell the police."

A dialogue like that was the last thing I wanted. So I said meekly, "I'm still curious, Leif. What is John after this time?"

"It is a reasonable question," Leif conceded. "You must realize, however, that the information is classified."

"Don't tell me Mr. Smythe has gone into espionage. He used to specialize in art."

"Oh, yes, that is his expertise. But it is a state secret, all the same."

"Give me a hint."

"I would be violating my oath as a police officer if I did that."

I could see his dilemma. I don't mean to disparage my ancestral homeland when I say there wasn't much in the entire country that was worth stealing. John didn't fool around with minor treasures, he went for the big stuff, the Mona Lisas and Koh-i-noors. Leif didn't even know enough about the Swedish collections to invent a believable lie; he must be aware that I knew more than he did.

I couldn't resist. I owed him one for insulting my intelligence with his inept fabrications and his macho love-making.

"Oh," I cried, as if enlightenment had suddenly dawned. "You don't mean . . . It isn't . . ."

Leif waited hopefully for me to finish. I just sat there, wide-eyed and fascinated.

Finally he said between his teeth, "Don't speak the word aloud. There are enemies everywhere."

"Naturally. But how is he going to do it?"

"If we knew for certain, we would not be so concerned."

"I wish I could help you."

"You can help me by dropping the subject," Leif said sincerely.

"But I'm intrigued. I can't believe even John would try . . . What a scandal it would cause!"

"Oh, yes." Leif was sweating. I decided to let him off the hook, not because I didn't enjoy watching him sweat, but because it was getting late. John might come or he might not; if he came, I wanted to be there in good time.

"Well, I hope you can tell me about it once the case is solved," I said, untangling myself from Leif and rising to my feet. "I'd better be getting back to the hotel now."

"Must you?" But he rose with alacrity, and offered me another stiff elbow.

As we walked along the flower-lined path, Leif said, "I did not answer your questions."

"I noticed that."

We left the park and stood on the corner waiting for the lights to change. Leif put his hand over mine. "You are no criminal. But I think you know more of this John Smythe than you have told me. Are you not aware that one of his confederates has followed us this evening?"

"You're imagining things. Unless it was one of your men—"

"He was no police officer. I saw him at the restaurant and also at the park—a short, very fat man, with large whiskers, wearing a straw hat."

The light changed. Leif towed me across the street.

I had kept an eye out for followers, but I was looking for brown beards, not bushy whiskers, and for a familiar profile, however garbed. The man Leif had seen might have been John. I discounted the description; anyone under six and a half feet tall might seem short to Leif, and false whiskers and fat tummies are easily procurable.

"Why didn't you apprehend the miscreant?" I inquired.

"How could I prove what I suspected? It is not a crime to be in the same places we are in." He added, "You do not seem alarmed. Do you know who it is that follows you?"

"You're the only one I know who is following me."

"Vicky, I beg you to tell me the truth," Leif said earnestly. "I only wish to protect you. Oh, I know the power a man like Smythe has over young and inexperienced females. You think he is romantic, *nicht?* He is handsome and brave, he robs only the rich. But he will break your heart—he will throw you on the trash, like a wilted flower."

Nobody, not even my father, who thinks I am still six years old, has ever pictured me as a fragile blossom. The image had a certain eccentric charm. It was also hysterically funny, the crowning masterpiece of all the antiquated clichés with which Leif had favored me that evening. My efforts to suppress a shriek of laughter resulted in convulsive muscular spasms and a series of gurgling noises.

Leif looked at me in alarm. "Do not break down until we reach your room. You will tell me all. It will relieve you."

I couldn't hold it in any longer. I reeled across the lobby and leaned on the desk, my face hidden in my hands and my shoulders heaving.

"She is not well," Leif explained to the mystified concierge. "Pay no attention. I will escort her to her room."

"No, you won't." I recovered in time to grab the key, which the concierge was offering to Leif. "I'm fine, I'm perfectly all right. Good night, Leif. Thanks for a very entertaining evening."

"But—" Leif began.

"No buts. I appreciate your efforts to protect me from myself. . . ." The image of the flower on the trash heap flashed onto my mental screen. The flower was a petunia—a wilted purple petunia. I covered my mouth with my hand and ran for the elevator.

By the time I reached my room my amusement had faded. Leif couldn't be that dumb. Nobody could be that dumb. Who the devil was he, anyway, and what did he want? He didn't fit into the scenario I had constructed earlier. The fat man who had been following us was another extraneous character. He might be a figment of Leif's imagination, designed to frighten me into confidentiality. If so, he was a singularly unconvincing invention; I'd have expected Leif to come up with something far more sinister. Please, God, I prayed silently—make John keep that appointment. Once I got my hands on that sneaky devil, I'd hold on to him until he came clean.

He was late. It was almost one A.M. before I heard the signal. I picked up one of the table lamps and held it poised as I opened the door.

John slid into the room and closed the door. Except for

red hair and a heavy tan, he had made no attempt to disguise himself.

"Aunt Ingeborg, I presume," I said.

"Damn." John kept a wary eye on the lamp. "So you've spoken with Gustaf. I hoped you hadn't."

"Why? Wasn't getting me and Gustaf together the point of this whole exercise?"

"Would you mind putting that lamp down?"

"I'd like to put it down on your head. Sit—over there, where I can keep an eye on you. And then talk. I want to know everything."

He didn't sit down. He kept shifting his weight, like a fighter who expects attack from several directions at once.

"I've only one thing to say, Vicky. I'll say it as succinctly as possible, and then I'm off. Go back to Munich. Catch the first plane tomorrow."

He was reaching for the doorknob when I brought the lamp down on his arm. Out of consideration for the hotel and my depleted traveler's checks I didn't hit as hard as I wanted to, but it was hard enough to make John pull his hand away. I got my back against the door.

"Talk," I said. "You went to a lot of trouble to set this up. However, your confederate in the States isn't very up-to-date. Aunt Ingeborg died eight months ago."

A shadow of vexation crossed John's face. It was replaced by a much livelier expression. "Vicky, this is no time to discuss my organizational problems. Matters have gone awry—decidedly awry. The deal is off. Canceled, kaput, finis, finito. Is that precise enough for you?"

"You're scared stiff," I said. "My God, you have your nerve, you bastard. Dragging me into a situation that terrifies you out of your wits, like a damned sitting duck—"

"Christ Almighty, do you think I'd have brought you

here if I had known what was going to happen?" We were yelling at each other, our faces only inches apart; his cheeks and forehead shone with a thin film of perspiration. "I didn't realize *he* was involved. My informant must have double-crossed me—sold the information twice—"

"If you don't mention a name pretty soon, I am going to call the police," I said, brandishing the lamp. "Who are you talking about? Leif?"

"Who the devil is Leif?" He jumped a good inch off the floor as a heavy fist hit the door right next to him.

"He is the very tall, very blond character who is beating on the door," I said. "I think I'll let him in. He visualizes me as a frail, wilted flower."

Treading lightly, John moved away from the door.

"I wonder what he has to do with this."

"You don't know? He isn't the man you're so scared of?"

"I haven't the vaguest notion who he is." John was capable of lying with extreme skill, but this time I believed him. He was too nervous to do a good job of prevarication.

Leif kept pounding on the door. He seemed to be under the delusion that he was doing it quietly, for in between bangs he kept repeating, "Let me in, Vicky, or I will make a loud noise. I know he is in there."

John sat down and folded his hands primly on his knee. "Police?" he inquired.

"He says he is. I doubt it."

"Hmph."

"Vicky, let me in!"

"If you don't stop that, I'm going to call the concierge," I shouted.

The banging stopped. After a moment Leif announced, "I will not go away. I will stay here all night."

"He probably will," I said to John. "Shall I call the desk?"

"The less attention we attract, the better."

"I have already attracted far too much attention."

"True. How do you find these people?"

I started to make a rude remark, but John cut me off. "The longer I stay, the worse for you, Vicky. You had better admit the irate gentleman. Once he's satisfied I'm not here, he'll leave. Or will he?"

I ignored the insolent leer that accompanied the question. "You are here," I said stupidly.

"I won't be when you let him in."

There was only one other exit from the room—the window.

"You can't," I exclaimed.

"How tall did you say Leif is? Seven feet? I assume he is proportionately broad, and he is obviously proportionately irate."

"Wait." I grabbed his arm as he strolled toward the window. "I'll telephone—the police, the manager—"

"And Leif the Lucky will broadcast my presence to half the population of Stockholm." I continued to tug at him as he paced; he glanced at me in surprise and then put two and two together. His eyes narrowed with amusement.

"Why, darling, I didn't know you cared. Do you really suppose I'm stupid enough to climb out that window?"

"Then what—"

"It's quite simple, really. Watch."

He pulled away from my grasp and headed for the door.

"Wait a minute," I exclaimed. "You can't walk out of here without telling me—"

"The less you know, the better for you. Get out, go home, depart."

"Damn it, John, what about Cousin Gustaf?"

He stopped. "Cousin Gustaf will be all right."

"You involved him too. You're after something he has. He told me himself he doesn't like strangers—so you planned to use me, a fictitious relative, to gain access to him. If your informant sold someone else the same information that led you to Gus, and that someone is less chickenhearted than you . . ."

In a very quiet, controlled voice, John said, "Bloody hell."

Leif started throwing himself against the door. Every object in the room rattled.

"What about Cousin Gus?" I insisted.

John swung around to face me. "Vicky, you don't get the picture. Gus is in no danger. At least . . . No, he can't be. The—er—the object of my present quest . . . Let me put it this way. Gus doesn't know where it is. I don't know exactly where it is myself. The 'someone' to whom you refer knows even less than I do. He can't . . . That is, he wouldn't . . ." His voice trailed off. After a moment he repeated, "Bloody hell."

"You can't even convince yourself," I said angrily. "Why the hell don't you tell me what you're after, instead of playing games?"

"The less you know, the better," John said again. "All right, damn it—I'll look after Gus. I promise."

"Ha, ha, ha," I said.

The door continued to rattle. I couldn't imagine why no one had complained. The people in the nearby rooms must be out.

John grabbed me by the shoulders and shook me. "I must have been out of my mind to bring you into this," he snarled. "You've brought me nothing but bad luck from first to last—"

"Well, who the hell asked you—" I began.

He stopped my mouth with his. The kiss lacked the leisurely finesse of his normal technique; it was hard and angry. When he let me go he was scowling. "I said I'd look after Gus, and I will. I'll keep my promise, even if it brings me to a sticky end, which it probably will. That should please you."

I saw no point in denying it. "Who's the man you're afraid of?"

"The field director of one of the most unscrupulous gangs of art thieves in Europe. I don't know what he looks like, since I have sincerely endeavored to avoid making his acquaintance. However, he is said to have an unusual hobby."

"What hobby?" I asked. But I thought I knew.

John's hand seized the doorknob. He glanced at me over his shoulder. "He cuts silhouettes."

He twisted the knob and flung the door open. His timing was perfect. Leif barreled through the opening like the Cannonball Express, reeled across the room, hit the bed, and crashed down on it. The bed collapsed.

I looked out into the hall. There was no one in sight.

Chapter Five

 COULD HAVE saved myself a lot of bother if I had mentioned Cousin Gustaf's name to the hotel management. The arrival of his Mercedes brought all the higher-ups out of their offices, bowing and smiling and hoping I had enjoyed my stay. Nobody mentioned the bed.

I wasn't ready when the car came. I didn't get to sleep until after two A.M. Leif tore the room apart. John had departed with such celerity that Leif hadn't laid eyes on him, and the big oaf refused to accept my statement that I was not concealing someone in the room. He made havoc among the clothes in the closet and stripped the bed down to the mattress. It took me half an hour to get things in order after he finally stormed out, muttering threats and dire warnings of disaster.

More than once, as pillows went flying across the room

and blouses tumbled off their hangers, I was tempted to ask why he didn't call in his cohorts from the Department of Art and Antiquities. I controlled the impulse for the same reasons that had kept me silent earlier. After the first quick survey of the room he must have known there wasn't anyone there; throwing blankets around was just his way of letting off steam.

I propped up the bed as best I could, but it wasn't very stable.

I was up at eight sharp. After a quick breakfast I headed for the museum, and argued my way into the office of the director. My official card gained me admittance to the library, though the place wasn't supposed to be open to the public till later.

I had some idea of what I was looking for, but even so it took a long time to find it. I kept wandering off into side tracks, some unexpectedly productive, others of purely academic interest. I took a lot of notes, though it was not necessary; the things I discovered had a poignant immediacy that branded them onto my memory.

Delayed by my research and by some last-minute shopping, I was still packing my suitcases when the phone rang and an awed voice announced that Herr Jonsson's car was waiting. Three bellboys arrived to carry my two suitcases. The third tried to take my purse, which was admittedly large enough to warrant his interest, but I insisted on carrying it myself.

In stately procession, amid ranks of bowing officialdom, we passed through the lobby. I loved it, especially when I caught a glimpse of Leif hiding behind a pillar, bent almost double in his attempt to look shorter. He rose to his full height, gaping, when he saw my entourage. I waved. A few discreet inquiries would tell him where I was going, but I figured it would take him a while to get on the trail. It was unlikely that he had a car, or he would have used it before this.

The chauffeur, a solemn middle-aged man, swept off his cap and handed me an envelope. I started to stuff it into my pocket. He frowned anxiously and said, "Please —read. . . ." So I did. The minuscule script covered the entire page; the text consisted solely of repetitive statements as to the reliability of Tomas and the happiness of Gus at my condescending to visit him.

The car lacked ostentatious gadgetry—TV sets, bars, and the like—but every appointment was of the best quality, and a pair of large baskets on the back seat showed that Gus had attempted to supply any missing amenities. As the car glided smoothly along the waterfront and across the bridge, I investigated the baskets. One was full of food—salads, sandwiches, and thermoses of various liquids; from white wine to mineral water— enough to feed a dozen people. The other basket contained a mirror, several magazines in three languages, a jug of water with rose leaves floating in it (presumably for washing, since a towel was wrapped around it), a supply of hand cream and cold cream, a miniature tape player with a selection of tapes (Bach and Vivaldi), a book of crossword puzzles and a freshly sharpened pencil, and a guidebook entitled *Beautiful Dalarna.*

By the time I had explored the baskets we were in the suburbs, heading northwest. I waited till the car stopped at a traffic signal before I banged on the glass. Tomas glanced back. I waved a sandwich at him. He smiled and shook his head. "Thank you. I have eaten." His voice came from over my head. As I might have expected, there was a speaker system between front and back seat.

I leaned back against the gray velvet upholstery and poured myself a glass of wine. The ride was so smooth that the pale gold liquid scarcely rippled when I placed the glass on the small table (rosewood, what else?) that unfolded from the armrest. I began to hope that Gus really was a cousin. Or that I could persuade him to adopt me. If I hadn't already been in love with him, the contents of those baskets would have won my heart.

The guidebook told me little that I didn't already know. I had looked up Karlsholm on a large-scale map at the museum that morning. It was too small to appear on the tourist map I had brought from Munich. It was in the county of Dalarna—Dalecarlia, Järnbäraland of the sagas—haunting, musical names, like something out of Tolkien. After all, northern history and legendry had inspired much of *The Lord of the Rings.* Dalecarlia might have been the hobbit name for the Elvish Dalarna, and it sounded like the sort of place hobbits would favor—a land of fertile farmland and green forest, of hills and rivers and deep-blue lakes. In the days of my innocence, before hordes of sinister characters started following me, I had planned to visit Dalarna. It is one of the few places in the world that is almost as charming as the guidebooks say it is.

Karlsholm was off the beaten track, some miles northwest of the popular tourist centers around Lake Siljan. It had a lake of its own, though; on the large-scale map Lake Vippen looked artificially symmetrical, like a small blue coin. The guidebook Gus had supplied didn't mention it, or the town, but there were references to the delightful folk costumes and customs, the crafts and the dances and the traditions of a past age lovingly preserved. Under the heading "Midsummer in Dalarna," the book waxed lyrical—cloudberries and cow horns, maypoles decked with wild flowers and birch branches, dancing to the sound of fiddles through the bright night hours of Midsummer's

Eve. That date was less than a week away. Maybe, if I could clean up the present mess, I would be able to celebrate the festival with Gus and the good villagers of Karlsholm. Footing it lightly around the maypole with a tall, handsome Swede. . . .

If I could clean up the mess. With a sigh I closed the guidebook and turned my thoughts from cloudberries to crime. I had most of the information I needed now. The only question was what to do with it.

Once upon a time—in 1889, to be precise—a hard-working farmer dug up a fabulous ancient treasure—the Karlsholm chalice. I'm not talking about Viking loot; the chalice dates from the so-called Migration Period, three to four hundred years before the Vikings. It was an enormously wealthy era in Scandinavia. As one authority said, the whole period glitters with gold—gold ingots and bars, gold coins, neck rings, and collars. Most of it was buried and never retrieved, possibly because its owners failed to return from their next raid on the dying Roman Empire, whence much of the treasure had come in the form of loot or tribute or ransom. One estimate stuck in my mind—the amount of gold used in the famous *lurs,* or horns, was worth about 1650 Roman solidi—the ransom of two hundred legionnaires.

The *lurs* came from Jutland, in Denmark, and the most interesting thing about them is that they were found, by accident, in the same field—a century apart.

I felt fairly sure I was dealing with a parallel case. The Karlsholm chalice was found in 1889. Almost a hundred years later someone unearthed another object in the same field—a field belonging to Gustaf Jonsson. A farmer, less honest than the majority of his countrymen, or a professional archaeological thief, following up a clue—I might never know, and it wasn't important. What was important was that the finder tried to sell his discovery to John, who enjoyed a certain reputation in his own slimy world.

I had never checked John's professional qualifications (it would have been a little difficult, since I didn't know his real name), but apparently he knew his subject well enough to have arrived at the same conclusion I had: Where there were two treasures, there might be more. Excavation of the site could produce a hoard like the one found in Södermanland, which contained more than twelve kilos of gold. Naturally, the real value of ancient jewelry is considerably higher than the value of the gold itself—worth a little trouble on John's part.

Investigating, he had learned that the site was owned by a wealthy, rigidly honest old gentleman who was disinclined to get matey with strangers. John's reputed charm wouldn't have the slightest effect on Gus. He had had to find another means of access—me. Anyone of Scandinavian descent is likely to have an ancestor named Johnson, or one of its variants.

John obviously knew a lot more about me than I knew about him. Since I had nothing to hide, my family history and connections would be easy to discover. So "Aunt Ingeborg" had written Gus, suggesting a meeting with her niece, and if I had gone to the hotel John selected for me, Gus would have called me. Except for the inconvenient demise of Aunt Ingeborg, I might have believed the story. She had been my great-aunt, actually, and an interfering old busybody. It would have been just like her to make appointments for me without bothering to ask whether I wanted to keep them. I had written Mother about my intention of traveling to Sweden. There would have been time—barely enough time—for Ingeborg to notify Gus of my plans.

Once I was in residence at Gus's home in Karlsholm,

John would move in. I wondered how he had planned to do it. Surely not the hoary old car-breakdown trick; he was more inventive than that. It was all rather chancy, but that was typical of John. No doubt he had several tentative approaches worked out.

However, his informant had crossed him up, peddling the information in several markets simultaneously. One such market was the one run by the silhouette cutter. It was strange how drastically John's disclosure had altered my impression of the little man, from that of a harmless eccentric to a figure of sinister villainy, snip-snipping away with his sharp-pointed scissors, reducing a human face to a flat black outline.

I wondered if it had occurred to John, as it had most certainly occurred to me, that the silhouette cutter might not be the only other source the informant had approached. The man who had socked John on the jaw, the mysterious person with the brown beard and horn-rimmed glasses, might be another treasure hunter. John didn't seem desperately worried about this character. I had never caught so much as a glimpse of him.

Then there was Leif. He seemed too naive and bumbling to be a professional criminal or a policeman. But he definitely wanted John, and not to buy him a schnapps. And what about the fat man with the whiskers, whom Leif claimed to have seen the previous night? For all I knew, every crook in Europe might be on my trail.

The others were more or less extraneous, at this point; one villain is one too many, and there was no question but that the silhouette cutter had spotted me. I remembered him sitting at the restaurant table, his gray head bent humbly over his work, his bright blades glinting. He had kept a copy of my portrait for himself. Perhaps one day it would adorn the wall in his private office, along with other black outlines commemorating his victims. The silhouette he had given me might have an equally eerie significance—an omen, a warning to those who understood its dark meaning.

John's consternation had unquestionably affected me. I have said John was a coward, and he was—a careful, calculating coward, who backed away from trouble with celerity and without hysterics. If the silhouette cutter scared him that much, I was scared too. And that was why I was on my way to Karlsholm. A man of Gus's wealth and prestige would be able to protect himself; he probably knew the King personally. But first he had to be convinced of the danger, and it wasn't the sort of danger one can explain over the telephone to a comparative stranger.

We stopped for lunch at a pretty inn on a blue lake. Having eaten a dozen smoked-salmon sandwiches (they were small sandwiches), I protested, but Tomas indicated, with sidelong looks and some hemming and hawing, that he had been directed to make periodic stops. I guess both he and his employer thought "bathroom" a vulgar word.

As the afternoon wore on, our deliberate pace began to get on my nerves. I didn't suggest that Tomas drive faster; I assumed Gus had ordered him not to joggle the merchandise. Under different circumstances I would have enjoyed the leisurely drive. The scenery was lovely—blue lakes set like jewels amid wooded hills, forest of birch and pine, red farmhouses with hand-carved gables, stretches of beach with healthy-looking brown bodies lying in rows like herring—doing just what I had planned to do on my holiday. Replete with sandwiches and wine, I dozed off. It had been a hard night.

When I woke up the sun had disappeared, and the skies were a depressing gray. We stopped again at a restaurant outside Mora, on Lake Siljan. I tactfully had tea, in order to give Tomas time to do whatever he wanted to do. It was after five. Gus had optimistically underestimated the length of time the drive would take. A fast driver could have done it in five or six hours, but we had been chugging along at a steady fifty, far less than that superb automobile was capable of doing. A glance at my map reminded me that Dalarna is a good-sized region, stretching all the way to the Norwegian border. Karlsholm was in the far northwest corner. We still had a way to go.

It may have been the change in the weather that induced a vague apprehension, formless as the clouds that hung overhead. I began to regret that I had not gone to the police before I left Stockholm. At the time it had not seemed the most practical solution. It is difficult to convince a stolid bureaucracy to take one seriously, especially with a story as wild as mine. I'd have done it in time; my credentials are impeccable, and I could have dragged in Schmidt and my buddies in the Munich police force. But it takes most men, including policemen, quite a while to get past my physical characteristics. Thirty-eight, twenty-six, thirty-six, if you must know. I'm not proud of them; they have been a distinct handicap to me throughout my life. I'm a historian, not a centerfold.

As I was saying, I had decided it would be easier to convince Cousin Gus and let him argue with the cops, especially since I wasn't absolutely certain I was right. My reasoning made good sense to me, but I had very little solid evidence with which to back it up. All the same, as I sipped my tea and stared at the shadowy outlines of the high hills ahead, I regretted my decision. Too late now.

Shortly after leaving the restaurant we turned off the modern highway onto a side road that twisted across the hills. It got narrower and more winding, dipping and rising again between aisles of birches whose black-striped trunks resembled processional pillars set up by a modern architect. Now and then the trees thinned out, giving views of upland meadows and barns like those of Austria and Switzerland, with steeply pitched roofs and solid, windowless walls. We were high in the hills now, in the *säter* country—the upland farms, where the cattle graze from Midsummer to Michaelmas. Huts and farmhouses, the heavy logs of their walls faded to a soft gray, clung tenaciously to the slopes.

Once Tomas had to pull far to the right to let a truck get past. We met little traffic; occasionally we passed hikers striding along with their backpacks jouncing. One turned and hoisted a hopeful thumb. Tomas didn't stop. The hitchhiker had brown hair and a beard. So did the male half of the next pair we overtook. The girl's bowed shoulders looked tired as she trudged along behind her companion. I leaned forward, then remembered the car was wired for sound. "I don't mind if you want to pick someone up, Tomas."

The peaked cap didn't turn. "No, miss. Not when you are here."

Gus's orders, no doubt. He must picture me as a fragile flower too. He was due for a shock when he saw me.

It was difficult to carry on a conversation with a disembodied voice and the back of a head. I was dying to pump Tomas about his employer, but doubted that he would indulge me. He didn't appear to be the gossipy type. I remembered a story I had once read that typified the sturdy independence of the people of this region. Some years back, when the crown prince was vacationing at Lake Siljan, he recognized a farmer who had been part of a delegation that had come to the palace. Thinking to make a gracious gesture, he sent an equerry to command the farmer to an audience. The farmer sent word back—

he was sorry, but he had to go to town to lay in his winter supply of liquor. If His Highness was still around, he might be able to get over to see him Thursday or Friday.

Between dense walls of fir and alder the road slipped down into a little clearing. A cluster of roofs and a bulbous wooden spire appeared, and Tomas said, "Karlsholm, miss. We are soon home."

I wondered where Gus's house could be. There was no sign of a mansion pretentious enough to match the Mercedes. The village was small—thirty or forty houses, a church, and a few larger structures that might have been public buildings. We passed through Karlsholm in about a minute and a half, even at a decorous pace, and climbed again. The car crested a low ridge.

Below lay the lake, almost as symmetrical in reality as it had been on the map—a steel-gray coin, dropped carelessly from an Ice Giant's pocket, encircled by somber groves and backed by the misty shapes of high mountains. But the map had not shown the island. It was shaped like a lopsided triangle, and at one end of it rose the black metal roof and white walls of a large house. Like the kings of Sweden, Gus had built his castle on his own private island.

Tomas stopped the car by a building near a small quay. It appeared to be a combination garage and boathouse, with a gas pump and shop. Sheltered by the overhang of the shop roof stood a row of chairs occupied by four or five elderly men looking as stiff and wooden as their seats. It made me feel right at home; there were always a few retired men with nothing better to do hanging around the gas station in Meadowbanks, Minnesota.

They were all tall and lean, with long, tanned faces and hair that could have been gray or bleached blond. A row of keen blue eyes studied me without blinking. Not a muscle cracked until I smiled and lifted a hand in greeting. Then five heads nodded in unison, but nobody smiled back.

A younger man wearing overalls came out of the shop, wiping his hands on a greasy rag. He was tall and blond and blue-eyed—it was getting monotonous, but that kind of monotony I can endure.

Tomas said, "My son, Erik." Apparently everybody was supposed to know who I was, but I said, "Hi, I'm Vicky Bliss," and held out my hand. Erik grinned and shrugged apologetically, indicating his grimy fingers. The old men watched stonily as Erik helped his dad unload a number of parcels from the car and stow them away in a neat little cabin cruiser. She was a beauty, and I'd love to have handled her, but I wasn't even allowed to stay up above. The minuscule cabin was as shipshape as the exterior; brass gleamed, mahogany shone, and a Formica-topped table held more magazines, bottles of beer, and mineral water, and a tray of open-faced sandwiches—caviar, this time.

Needless to say, the caviar and the beer were still intact when we docked. The trip took only about ten minutes.

I found myself on a windswept jetty with a flight of steep wooden steps ahead. Tomas gestured toward them, raising an inquiring eyebrow, and when I nodded he got back into the cockpit and started easing the boat toward a covered shed at the end of the jetty.

At the top of the steps a graveled path led through formal gardens to the front of the house. It looked even bigger close up than it had from a distance. Part creamy stucco, part gray weathered wood, part stone, it appeared to have grown over the centuries as naturally as the trees that sheltered it.

A man stood at the door looking eagerly in the direction

of the stairs, and when he started forward I understood why he had not met me at the dock. Even with the aid of his stout wooden stick he limped badly, dragging one foot.

I knew what his first words would be. "I am so happy! Come in, come in, you must be tired. It is a long journey."

He looked just the way I had pictured him—in fact, he looked like the five old gents at the garage, except for the smile that gave his lined face an inner radiance. Like many men of his coloring he had worn well; he might have been any age between forty and seventy, and with the exception of the bad leg he had kept in good shape.

With a wide, hospitable gesture he showed me into the house. The hallway was dark and narrow, with pieces of heavy furniture lined up in rigid rows. A doorway on the left led to a lighted room. I turned in that direction, but before I had taken more than a few steps, Gus said seriously, "Victoria, there is tragic news. Be brave, my child. It was so good of him to come the long distance to share your grief and give you the comfort of a friend and kinsman."

Heaven knows I have plenty of hostages to Fortune, starting with my parents and proceeding through a long line of friends and relatives; but it never occurred to me for an instant that there had been a genuine tragedy. After a moment's pause I went into the room. And there he was, the bastard, perfectly at ease, immaculately tailored, the one, the original, restored by the miracles of modern cosmeticians to his Anglo-Saxon fairness.

In a voice choked with emotion I quoted from the sagas. "Blonde was his hair and bright his cheek; Grim as a snake's were his glowing eyes. . . ."

"I hate to be the one to tell you, Vicky," John interrupted. "Aunt Ingeborg is—is—"

"Dead," I agreed. "You know, for some strange reason I'm not surprised to hear it."

John swept me into a brotherly embrace. He looks so willowy and aristocratic, I keep forgetting how strong he is. One arm squashed my ribs and cut off my breath, the other hand pressed my face into his shoulder. As I squirmed, unable to utter a word, he said to Gus, "A glass of brandy, perhaps? The shock, you know."

Gus clucked sympathetically and hurried out. Freeing my mouth, I mumbled an obscenity into John's tweed shoulder. He kept his hand firmly on my head.

"I told you I'd look after Gus," he murmured. "Why the devil didn't you do as I asked?"

I said, "Let go of me."

The pressure on my neck subsided so that I was able to move my head. John promptly kissed me, with considerably more skill than he had displayed the night before.

"Nice," he said, as I sputtered. "You really have the most—"

"What have you told Gus?"

"Nothing. I thought I'd leave that to you. You can be so much more persuasive."

"I'm telling him the truth."

"You don't know the truth. I don't doubt that your educated guesses are reasonably accurate, but we ought to discuss the situation before deciding what to say. If you give me your word not to accuse me—"

"Why should I let you off the hook?"

"I've no intention of being keelhauled over this deal," John said, with a glint in his eye that told me he meant every word. "If you cooperate, I can be of considerable assistance. If you won't—"

Before he could complete the threat, I heard Gus's footsteps approaching. Another pair of feet accompanied his, in a quick pitter-patter. They belonged to a stout old lady carrying a tray with glasses and decanter.

I wrenched myself away from John. "I'm fully recovered, thank you," I said.

"You are very courageous," said Gus, viewing my flushed face and disheveled hair with the respect such signs of grief deserved.

"She had a good life," I said. "Ninety-six years old and not a tooth missing."

John showed signs of breaking down—or up—at that point, so brandy was administered all around and everybody cheered up. Gus introduced his housekeeper, Mrs. Andersson, who displayed a mouthful of artificial teeth as impressive as Aunt Ingeborg's and bade me welcome in a mixture of Swedish and English. For the next few minutes she ran in and out with trays and plates and little doilies to put under the plates and little tables to put under the plates and doilies.

John won the housekeeper's heart by devouring her canapés and paying her extravagant compliments that made her giggle and blush. I couldn't eat. I was too choked with rage.

John must have left Stockholm early that morning. I wasn't impressed or touched by his apparent fidelity to his promise. I felt sure that protecting Gus wasn't his only purpose in coming.

By catching me off guard, he had won the first round. I should have yelled for the police instead of appearing to accept him; now any accusations I might make would be weakened. Most galling of all was my suspicion that by hook or by crook, by gosh and by golly, he had somehow maneuvered me into the precise position he had meant me to occupy from the first. If my analysis of the situation was correct, there was only one way out of the dilemma

John had gotten us into, and that was to do what he had always intended to do—dig up the field and find whatever might be there before illicit investigators could get to it.

His supposedly casual comments supported this conclusion. The conversation had turned to the house and its architectural features, its fine antique furnishings and decor. John babbled fluently about Dalarna baroque and eighteenth-century design. Gus looked impressed.

"You are a student of art, Mr. Smythe?"

"That's one word for it," I said.

"Archaeology is my specialty," John said. "I couldn't help noticing the earthworks behind the house, Mr. Jonsson. They resemble the remains of hill forts found in other parts of Sweden. Have you ever thought of excavating?"

"There are ancient remains there," Gus said. "My grandfather made a hobby of agriculture; wishing to try a new variety of grass, he ordered the upper pasture to be plowed, and one of the workmen turned up some sort of cup. Grandfather presented it to a museum in Stockholm."

"Of course," John exclaimed, his eyes wide. "The Karlsholm chalice. I know it well."

"I am told it is a fine piece," Gus said indifferently.

"It is magnificent. Sir—haven't you ever wondered whether there might not be other antiquities buried there?"

"If they are there, they will remain there," Gus said. "I won't have archaeologists tramping over my island desecrating the graves of my ancestors."

John gave me a meaningful glance, meaning, "You see what I was up against?" I snorted. Gus asked if I had taken cold.

Shortly after we moved into the dining room, for a

wholly unnecessary meal, it began to rain. Water streamed down the windowpanes like something out of a celestial fire hose. Glancing at the impressive display, John said, "I'm most grateful for your invitation to stay the night, sir. I'd hate to drive those roads in this sort of weather."

"Yes, we have very violent storms," Gus said proudly. "In winter I am often cut off for days at a time. I have my own generator for electricity, but always when it rains the telephone does not function."

I did not need John's sidelong smirk to tell me that the weather had put another spoke in my wheel. There would be no telephone call to the police tonight. I hadn't expected I would get that far in one evening; older people are hard to convert to a new point of view, especially as one as hard to swallow as the tale I meant to tell. I'd have a better chance of persuading Gus of the danger with John to back me up; that expert and congenital liar undoubtedly had concocted a modified version of the facts that would convince Saint Peter, while leaving "Sir" John in line for a halo.

As soon as he decently could, Gus turned the conversation to genealogy. He seemed puzzled by John's and my relationship.

"Distant cousins," John said airily, when the question was put. "Vicky's grandmother's sister was my grandfather's brother's second wife."

Even the expert genealogist was baffled by that one.

After dinner we went to Gus's study, a room the size of a football field, lined with bookcases and equipped with comfortable chairs. Tables and desks were covered with papers—Gus's genealogical materials. His eyes alight, his face beaming, Gus outlined the history of "our" family back to the creation of the world. It was rather interesting, or it would have been if I had not had other things on my mind. At any rate, Gus enjoyed himself. He might be a recluse but he was also a fanatic, and every fanatic loves an audience.

He kept thinking of things he wanted to show us—a faded satin slipper that had belonged to a lady-in-waiting of Queen Christina, the sword an ancestor had carried at Narva. After watching him hoist himself painfully out of his chair a time or two, John offered his services; Gus kept him running back and forth to fetch more souvenirs, which were tucked away in cupboards under the book-cases. While John was scrounging in one such cupboard at the far end of the room looking for the birth certificate of a seventeenth-century Jonsson, Gus turned to me.

"Mr. Smythe," he whispered. "He is not—are you per-haps—your relationship is . . ."

"We're just friends." I gagged on the word, but Gus didn't notice. He looked relieved.

"I am so glad. He is a very pleasant young man, I have no prejudice, believe me; but there is something—I cannot say what . . ."

I was strongly tempted to tell him what. There wasn't time. John trotted back with the birth certificate and we spent the rest of the evening on family history. I have never heard such lies as John told when Gus started in-quiring about the English and American branches.

When the mellow tones of the old clock in the corner boomed eleven times, Gus rose. "Come with me to the window, Vicky," he said.

The sun had dipped below the far mountains, outlining their snowcapped heights in molten gold. The storm had left a path of broken clouds, like bloody footsteps running down the west. The shore lay deep in shadow, a slope of unbroken green whose reflection deepened the water to dark malachite.

"I stand here each night," Gus said quietly. "Before I go to bed. Each night it is different, each night it is beautiful. You must see it in winter, Vicky, when every tree is trimmed in ermine and the full moon turns the snow to silver."

"I can see why you love it," I said.

"It is part of your heritage too. I am so glad you are here to share it with me."

"Mr. Jonsson," I blurted, "there's something I have to tell you—"

"You must call me Gus. Cousin Gus."

"That's very sweet of you, but I want to tell you—"

"I don't think this is the time, Vicky," said John, close behind me.

"No, it is late," Gus agreed. "You will be weary from your journey."

He escorted us to our rooms. They were on the ground floor in a separate wing. I had seen mine when I went to wash up before dinner, but I had not realized that Gus's room was next to mine and that John had been given a room at the far end of the corridor—with Gus's door between.

"I bid you good-night," Gus said, standing tall in his doorway. "I am a light sleeper, so if there is anything you require in the night, do not hesitate to call me."

As if that weren't enough of a hint, he continued to stand there with the look of a man who is prepared to remain in the same spot all night.

"Good night, sir," John said. He looked at me. Gus looked at me. Neither of them moved until I had closed my door.

If I had kept my wits about me, I could have invented a valid reason for a private interview with John—vague references to "family matters" would have done it. Gus's old-fashioned notions of chaperonage did me in; I was too entertained to think quickly, and once those bedroom doors were closed, the die was cast. The dignified, lovable old man intimidated me. He wouldn't say anything if he caught me sneaking into John's room in the middle of the night, but he would be disappointed and hurt and disapproving.

Excuses, excuses. It's easy to think of them once the damage is done. I didn't have any sense of urgency. The physical isolation of the island gave me a feeling of security, and John's relaxed air implied that he had no fear of immediate pursuit. I had even begun to wonder whether the far-out story about the criminal conspiracy and the fiendish silhouette cutter might not be an invention of John, and his attempt to get me to go back to Munich an example of reverse psychology. I definitely had to talk to the rat, but morning would be soon enough. I would corner him first thing, when I was rested and calm and better able to deal with his lies.

Like so many good intentions, that one now forms a paving block on the road to the bad place. In fact, a considerable stretch of that path owes its solidity to me. It is small consolation to reflect that even if I had acted on my instincts instead of trying to behave calmly, things would have turned out just the same.

Chapter Six

WAS AWAKENED once during the night by a strange, high-pitched cry. It was not repeated. I concluded I must have been dreaming, but I was sufficiently concerned to get out of bed and go to the door.

Dim lights burned in the hall. Gus's door was slightly ajar. His room was dark, but as I listened I heard faint rustling noises, like someone turning over in bed. That put an end to any idea I might have had of seeking a midnight rendezvous with John. So I went back to bed. Not that it would have made any difference. . . .

It was a little after five when I was awakened for the second time, and on this occasion the noises could not be mistaken for the products of my imagination. Crashes, thuds, and curses echoed through the house.

Like the fool that I am, I dashed into the hall. The noises came from John's room. Gus's door was now closed; either he was up and about, or he was a heavier sleeper than he had claimed, for he did not appear.

John's door was open. By the time I reached it, the noises had stopped. The room was a disaster—furniture overturned, sheets torn off the bed, and a handsome lamp smashed to bits. At the foot of the bed, sprawled in awkward abandon, was a body. It was that of a man with longish brown hair, wearing a dirty white sweater and faded jeans. A pair of horn-rimmed glasses, miraculously unbroken, lay on the floor by his hand. Over him, breathing heavily and dripping blood from a split lip, stood John.

I hadn't quite taken all this in, much less absorbed the full effect of John's pale-blue silk pajamas with the gold crest on the pocket, when the muslin curtains exploded into the room and another man appeared. There was no mistaking his identity. It was fully light outside, and he filled the entire window embrasure. His eyes bulged, and his hair bristled like that of an antique warrior in the grip of the insane berserker rage. After one quick glance, from the recumbent body to John, he let out an animal howl and flung himself forward.

His shoulders stuck in the window. The delay gave John time enough to leap aside. Leif stumbled forward, assisted by John's foot, and hit the floor with a crash that shook the room. One of his outflung arms sent me reeling backward. I bounced off the wall and sat down harder than I wanted to.

John appeared to be a trifle put out, but he had not lost his grasp on essentials. He snatched up a heavy brass candlestick and headed for Leif, who was grunting and gasping and trying to get his wind back. I scrambled to my feet and wrapped myself around John in time to stop the blow.

"What do you think you're doing?" he gasped, trying to free his arm. "I want to—"

"I know what you want." He got his left hand free. Leif struggled to his knees, shaking his head dizzily. John curled his fingers into his palm and hit me under the ear. I sat down again. Leif sat up. John weighed the new developments and opted for flight. He was halfway to the door when a fresh complication appeared.

The man was pretty big, but not as big as Leif. In this case, however, size did not matter. He'd have been just as effective if he had been four feet tall. He pointed the gun at John and said, "Halt."

John halted. The man with the gun advanced into the room. John retreated, tactfully avoiding Leif and the body, which was making uncouth noises and jerking its limbs. A second man followed, also carrying a gun.

"Mais quel contretemps," he remarked, surveying the chaos. *"Qu'est-ce qui s'est passé?"*

"Die Kerle haben sich geschlagen," his companion explained. *"Was sollen wir mit ihnen anfangen?"*

"Je demanderai."

He went out.

The body rolled over. It was the man John had described. He looked deathly ill, his cheekbones jutting sharply, his skin sallow. When he opened his eyes the nature of his complaint was evident. They were red-rimmed and bloodshot. From his sagging mouth a trickle of saliva ran down into his matted beard.

I made a little noise of pity and revulsion. Leif lifted the limp body so that it was supported against his shoulder.

"Behold the work of your friend, whom you were so careful to protect," he said bitterly. "A pretty sight, *nicht?*"

John's stare held no pity, only disgust. With a shrug he

turned to the guard and said calmly, "I'd like to put on my dressing gown, Hansel. Watch that trigger finger, eh?"

The Frenchman returned. *"Là-bas, tout de suite,"* he said briskly.

I demanded my robe and was allowed to get it, with the Frenchman as an escort. They were quite an international crowd. I suppose I should have been scared, but everything had happened so fast, I couldn't take it in. All those people turning up out of nowhere. . . . There was only one character missing.

He was waiting for us in Gus's study, leaning back in the desk chair as if he were the owner of the house. He wore the thick gray wig, but he had replaced his sweater with an expensive-looking three-piece suit. As we were ushered into the room, he rose politely.

"A pleasure to see you again, Dr. Bliss. Will you join me for breakfast? The good housekeeper of Mr. Jonsson was kind enough to prepare it before she left, and I promise you it will be excellent."

The food was set out on a table by the window, doilies and all. Dazedly I sank into the chair the gray-haired man held for me.

"Perhaps I may impose on you to pour," he went on. "Gentlemen, don't be shy—take your places."

John was the first to obey. He kept a wary eye on Leif, but the latter was occupied with the man whose twitching, muttering body he supported.

"Where is Mr. Jonsson?" I asked.

The gray man smiled approvingly. "I am happy to see you accept the situation sensibly, Dr. Bliss. Mr. Jonsson is in our hands. He will be released unharmed as soon as we finish our work here—unless one of you does something foolish. At my request, he has given his staff a little holiday. He was easily persuaded to do so when I pointed out that their safety might depend on their ignorance of the situation. They are accustomed to his eccentricities, and unquestioningly accepted his statement that we will be engaged in certain experiments that require privacy and solitude."

"You seem to have thought of everything, Mr. . . . I don't know your name."

"Please call me Max. It is not my real name, of course, but that is the rule in this group; you are the only one of us who has not been traveling under a pseudonym."

"You mean Leif—" I began.

"Is a German engineer named Hasseltine," Max said. "The disgusting apparition he tends so lovingly is his brother Georg—once a promising young archaeologist."

They didn't look like brothers, but Max's explanation accounted for several things that had puzzled me. I said, "I should have known Leif wasn't your real name."

His hand on his brother's shoulder, he gave me a strained smile. "The friends of my youth sometimes called me that."

"I was pretty sure you weren't a Swede, though. You slipped a few times, used a German word."

"I am a simple man," Leif said simply. "Intrigue and deceit are not easy for me. I have business in Munich, that is how I knew of you, Vicky. I am ashamed I did not tell you the truth, but . . ."

He indicated his brother, who was mumbling in German and making ineffectual attempts to rise.

"I understand," I said.

Leif turned to Max. "I must take care of him. He wants his rucksack. He needs . . . He must have . . ."

"He does indeed." Max studied the mumbling object with dispassionate contempt. "Well, why not? Pierre—the luggage, please."

It was brought from our rooms—John's expensive matched calfskin bags, my battered plastic ditto, a big leather two-suiter, and a canvas backpack. At the sight of the latter Georg Hasseltine made sick, mewing noises. Max gestured. The Frenchman opened the pack and dumped its contents onto the floor.

In addition to the usual toilet articles and clothing, the bag contained two interesting items—a wicked-looking knife and a tin box that rattled when Max nudged it with a fastidious toe. Wrinkling his nose at the smell of dirty socks, Max snapped out directions. Pierre confiscated the knife; Leif got the box, and his brother. He carried both out of the room. The other objects were crammed back into the pack, and John's suitcases were brought forward. Pierre dropped them at Max's feet like a dog presenting his master with a fat rat.

There wasn't much left of the bags or their contents by the time Pierre finished searching them. He ripped seams and tore out linings with zealous pleasure. John winced every time a garment was desecrated; once he made a mild protest. "You know I never carry a weapon, Max. Have a heart. That shirt cost me—"

"What is this?" Max pounced on a monogrammed leather case.

"Hair dryer," John said, without even blushing.

"How decadent," Max muttered, adding it to the pile of confiscated objects—a set of ivory-handled razors, a pair of small dumbbells (whose evil significance eludes me to this day), and a manicure set exquisitely encoiffed in morocco leather and red plush, which included several lockpicks.

By contrast, my beat-up cases were handled with gentlemanly tenderness. The clothes I had unpacked the night before had been replaced in the suitcases—not too neatly, but I had no real cause for complaint, since I am a notoriously sloppy packer. Max inspected each garment, except for the underwear. Even his nasty, suspicious mind couldn't find anything remotely resembling a weapon in a pair of bikini panties. When he had finished with the suitcases, he reached for my purse.

A man can't understand why a woman's handbag is such a sensitive object—almost an extension of her person. I don't fully understand it myself. Maybe it's because we keep so many private, intimate possessions in our purses—love letters, cosmetics, jelly doughnuts. . . . Maybe a purse is a symbol of the womb, or something equally Freudian. I can't explain it, but I know I hate the idea of a stranger's hands rummaging in my bag. I had to bite back a yelp of protest when Max dumped the contents out onto the desk.

He made a few jokes, naturally. I suppose he thought they relieved the tension. He grinned and raised his eyebrows over the little black book in which I had, unwisely, made some personal comments beside certain addresses. Some of the cosmetics raised a ridiculous amount of mirth. What's so funny about eyelash curlers, for heaven's sake?

He was not so amused as to neglect his precautions. My Swiss pocket knife went into the *verboten* pile, along with my can of Mace. Occasionally he asked quizzically, "And what is the purpose of this item?" I snapped out answers. "Tape measure. In case I see a picture frame that might fit one of my prints. Stockings. In case I want to try on shoes. Sewing kit. In case I rip my clothes. Flashlight. Do I have to explain why I carry a flashlight?"

Leif's suitcase contained nothing of interest. He was allowed to keep his razor; it was electric.

The henchmen tossed our belongings back into the

suitcases. Then there was an expectant pause.

They searched John first. Hans's pudgy fingers went over every inch of his body. He didn't complain until Hans messed up his exquisitely brushed hair. "Damn it, Hansel. . . . Don't overlook anything, I beg. What about the cyanide pill and the teeny-tiny knife wedged between my back molars?"

He opened his mouth to its widest extent. Hans was actually peering into the cavity when Max snapped, "Enough."

All eyes turned toward me. I stood up and untied the belt of my robe.

Max said sharply, "Turn your backs."

The henchmen exchanged eloquent glances, but obeyed. "You, too," Max said to John. His face preternaturally grave, John executed a smart right-about wheel and stood at attention, the back of his ruffled head fairly radiating amusement.

I took off my robe. In deference to Gus I was wearing the least revealing of my nightgowns. It bared my shoulders and arms and my legs below the knee—well, actually, below mid-thigh.

Max studied the exposed parts of me with shrinking fastidiousness. He was clearly torn between personal distaste and professional thoroughness, so I decided to help him out.

"How's this?" I asked, bunching up the gown in back and pulling it tight against my front.

Max looked relieved. "Yes, that is adequate. If you will turn . . ."

He stayed behind the desk while I pivoted and pulled and adjusted the fabric. I suppose, in a way, it was a more perverse performance than stripping to the buff, and it certainly took longer, but I realized that in his own weird way Max believed he was respecting my maidenly modesty. He made me put my robe back on before he let the boys turn around.

Hans trotted out with the luggage and Max returned to the role of gracious host. He offered me a plate of pastries. I took one, but the first bite tasted like sand, so I put it on my plate. "Why are you going to all this trouble?" I asked bluntly. "I don't know what's out there, but unless you have more information than I do, you must know it can't be worth the time and trouble you will have to expend on it. Surely there are enough accessible objects, in museums and collections, to occupy your time, without resorting to excavation."

"Mr. Jonsson's pasture may prove more productive than you think," Max said. "However, you are quite right in your assessment. Under normal circumstances our organization deals only with products that are already on the market, so to speak. However, there are times when even a hard-headed businessman may be moved by personal motives."

The muscles of his neck stretched to a degree I had thought possible only in certain reptiles. His eyes focused on John.

John was expecting it. His hand was quite steady as he reached for his coffee cup. "Max, old chum—"

"You have annoyed us for a long time," Max said softly. "We expect and tolerate a certain amount of competition, but your methods go beyond the level of tolerance. This last affair—you made a fatal error, my friend. Now you have compounded it. Why did you not heed my warning?"

Over the rim of John's cup a pair of cornflower-blue eyes gazed soulfully at me. Before I could protest, Max murmured, "I wondered if that might not be the case."

"There is no reason for us to be at odds," John said. "I don't know what Albert told you—"

"Everything," said Max, closing his lips with a snap on the last syllable.

John went a shade paler. "I see."

"You mean you—" I began.

"Please, Dr. Bliss. Let us not dwell on distasteful subjects."

"Poor old Al," John muttered. "I knew him well. . . . Yes, but look here, Max. Al couldn't have given you a precise location, because he didn't have it. I've worked out a few theories that might help. That's a largish stretch of pasture; what do you say we collaborate?"

Max did not respond to this naive proposal. We were sitting in silence when the brothers Hasseltine returned.

I had seen "before" and "after" pictures, but the transformation in the younger man made me stare. He was still haggard and worn, but now his step was firm and his eyes were aware. The therapy that had cured Georg (only too temporarily) had had the reverse effect on Leif. When he saw John, he made a grating noise deep in his throat and started for him, hands flexing.

Max got between them. "Sit down, Mr. Hasseltine. I understand your feelings, but you must wait your turn. There is a chance he may yet be helpful to us."

"He does not deserve to live," Leif muttered. "He should die slowly, with the same agony he brought to others."

"No doubt he will." Max flicked an invisible speck of dust from his coat sleeve. "But not until he has served his purpose."

His icy calm had the desired effect. Leif's distorted face relaxed. "I don't know what you want here," he said slowly. "It is not my business. An enemy of Smythe is no enemy of mine—so long as you mean no harm to this lady and her friend."

"Excellent," Max said. "Let me make it quite clear, so there will be no unfortunate misunderstandings. None of you is to leave the island or attempt to communicate with the mainland. I hold Mr. Jonsson as security for your good behavior, Dr. Bliss; I feel sure you will not risk his safety by acting foolishly. You—" He looked at John. "You may try to escape. Please feel free to try."

John wasn't the only one to shiver at that speech. "I presume," he said, "that you will exterminate the others if one of us gets away. You count on the fact that I wouldn't abandon Dr. Bliss."

"Oh, I wouldn't count on that," I said earnestly to Max. "I really wouldn't."

"You underestimate yourself, my dear." His smile was paternal. "Do not fear; where Sir John is concerned, I count on nothing. I have other methods of controlling him. As for you two . . ."

"I have told you where I stand," Leif said. "This lady is hostage for me."

Georg had seated himself at the table and was wolfing down food. He looked up. "I haven't been exactly with it lately," he said coolly. "Just what are you after, Mr. — Max, is it?"

Max leaned back in his chair, fingertips together, and studied the speaker. Georg returned his gaze composedly. I wondered what he was hooked on. It was amazing stuff, whatever it was.

"Our project should interest you, Dr. Hasseltine," he said. "We have reason to believe that there is a fifth-century hoard of gold and silver buried in the pasture behind this house."

"Migration Period?" Georg looked interested. Then he

shrugged. "Not my field. I'm a classical archaeologist."

"But you have had excavation experience."

"Oh, certainly. I'm a first-rate excavator."

"I believe you."

"I suppose you want my help," Georg went on airily. "You're no archaeologist. I knew that as soon as I saw the fellows with the guns." He laughed heartily at his own wit.

"We could certainly use the assistance of a scholar with your reputation," Max said. Leif winced, but Georg appeared not to notice the double entendre. He was flying high. With another cheery laugh he leaned over and clapped Max on the shoulder.

"Perhaps we can come to an agreement."

"Georg," Leif exclaimed. "Please—"

"Shut up!" Georg turned on him. "Always you interfere with me, always you play the big brother. Leave me alone. I know what I'm doing."

"Quite right," Max said. "Why don't you come with me, Dr. Hasseltine, and I will show you the site."

"Great." Georg tossed down a half-eaten roll and rose. Hans and Pierre followed the pair out.

"Now we escape," Leif said. "While they leave us unguarded."

John gave him a peculiar look. "He doesn't need to guard us, you idiot. He has us by the short hairs."

"He means what he says—that he will kill the old man?"

"He means it."

"Then we must free the old man."

"Splendid idea. Brilliant plan. How do you propose we go about it?"

"First," said Leif, "we must find where they are keeping him."

John sighed. "I'm going back to bed."

He sauntered out, his leisurely stride a calculated insult. Leif glowered at his retreating back. "Someday I smash his face."

"Max is planning to take care of that little matter for you," I said.

"And you object."

"I object to murder. It's just a silly girlish prejudice."

Sarcasm was wasted on Leif. He gave me a blank stare. "Besides," I went on, "we can't depend on Max's guarantees. How do we know he won't kill all of us when he's finished here?"

"Why should he?"

"Because he's a criminal," I said patiently. "His organization specializes in grand theft, blackmail, torture, and murder. For God's sake, Leif, you can't be that naive."

"Then what do you want to do?" Leif asked, frowning.

"Well, I sure as hell don't want to sit around waiting for Max to make up his mind whether or not to kill me."

"You wish to escape from him?"

"You've got it."

"All of us?"

"All of us."

"Smythe too?"

"Smythe too."

"You wish me to help?"

"That would be very nice."

Leif thought about it, stroking his mustache thoughtfully. Then he nodded. "Very well. First we find the old man. Then we escape—all of us, even Smythe. Then I smash Mr. Smythe's face."

Whereupon he left the room, having arranged his program to his satisfaction.

Aside from a few imponderables—such as locating Gus,

overpowering his guards, and knocking all the other villains unconscious—there was one basic flaw in Leif's
scheme. In a few brilliantly conceived sentences, Max had
made Georg a confederate. Perhaps Georg had once been
a promising archaeologist—his name was vaguely familiar—but Max had two firm holds on him now: the drug
he used, which Max could hand out or withhold at his
own discretion, and Georg's hatred of John. If he had been
chasing his bête noir all over Europe, he was not about to
shake hands and forget the whole thing. He'd be more
than happy to cooperate in Max's project of extermina-
tion, and although I didn't know the precise details of the
part John had played in his disintegration, I wasn't altogether sure I blamed him.

The coffee was cold. I swallowed the repulsive dregs
and decided I might as well get dressed. I hadn't had much
sleep, but there was no chance of wooing Morpheus, not
in my present mood.

My room was a shambles. Someone had done a thor-
ough job of searching it. Straightening up the mess gave
me a chance to work off some pent-up anger; it was also
a form of protest against the chaos these thugs had
brought into Gus's harmless, decent life.

I put on jeans and a long-sleeved shirt and tossed a
sweater over my shoulder. On my way out I passed John's
door and paused to listen. Not a sound. I eased the door
open. He lay curled up like a sleeping baby, an angelic
smile on his lips. His lashes, several shades darker than his
hair, fringed the closed lids with gold.

I slammed the door as hard as I could and went on.

The echoes of the slam followed me as I trotted along
the corridor, fighting a panicky impulse to run. The still-
ness of the empty house was unnerving. My brain

couldn't seem to get in gear. A succession of shocks had stunned it into stupidity.

Unless Max struck it lucky, I had a couple of days. He wouldn't dispose of us until he had no further use for us as hostages or sources of information. In fact, he might have been telling the truth when he said he meant to let us go unharmed. It wasn't as if we were the only people in the Western Hemisphere who could identify him as a master criminal. After due reflection I decided I had a seventy–thirty chance of survival. But I didn't like the odds. Where my life is concerned I prefer a sure thing.

There were two possible methods of procedure. The first was to rescue Gus and then go on from there. The second was to immobilize Max and all his gang. I am sure I need not explain why, after very brief consideration of the second idea, I returned to method number one.

Method number one depended on my assumption that Gus was somewhere on the island. If he had been transported to the mainland, the whole deal was off. But it would have been risky to move him in broad daylight, after he had announced to his staff that he was entertaining guests. Also, a smart crook like Max would want his hostage accessible, in case I demanded to see him or speak with him.

Assuming Gus was on the island, assuming I could find him and set him free—what next?

We could make a run for it, or we could call for help and hold the gang at bay until said help arrived. Holding the gang at bay meant hiding; I wasn't about to consider anything more adventurous. Gus must know some good hiding places. The burning question was: Could I contact the mainland?

Just for the hell of it, I tried the telephone. As I had

expected, it was dead. Gus probably had an emergency means of communication laid on—a shortwave or CB radio or something of that sort—and if I ever found Gus I would ask him. I decided not to waste time searching, though. Unless it was well concealed, Max had probably dealt with it already.

Smoke signals, setting the barn on fire, flashing SOS's with my pocket mirror . . . Too chancy. So much for the idea of communicating with the mainland. The alternative, running for our lives, presented one minor difficulty. We couldn't run. We were surrounded by water.

So far my reasoning hadn't been distinguished for brilliance or originality. If I couldn't do better than that, I might as well forget the whole thing.

The silence of the house was getting to me. I headed for the door. It was a relief to be in the sunlight and fresh air. The rain had left everything looking fresh and clean. The wind stung my face. I assumed the thugs were all in the pasture, digging for treasure, but I kept a wary eye peeled as I descended the stairs to the dock. When the boathouse door opened, I got ready to duck. But it was only Leif.

"I have looked," he said. "Nothing we can use."

I was prepared for that discouraging statement; the fact that Max hadn't bothered to set a guard on the boats was proof positive that they had been put out of commission. Hope dies hard, though. When I advanced, Leif grinned and stood aside to let me see for myself.

The more I looked, the madder I got. Max hadn't just destroyed the boats, he had smashed the dreams and memories they symbolized. In his younger days Gus must have been a first-class mariner. Now the canoe and the kayak and the neat little sailboat lay deep underwater, held only by their mooring ropes. The rowboat was a utility craft, big enough to hold several people and a tidy

amount of cargo. At least it could have held them if someone hadn't chopped a hole in the bottom. The cruiser
appeared to be undamaged, except for the shortwave,
which had been demolished.

I sat in the cockpit and swore.

Leif peered in at me. "The key is missing."

"I know."

"Perhaps there is another key."

"If we ever find Gus, we can ask him." I took Leif's
proffered hand and climbed out. "Isn't there some way of
starting her up without a key? I've done it with cars, but
I'm not familiar with this type of engine."

Leif shrugged, looking almost as bland and stupid as
Hans, and I snapped, "I thought you were an engineer."

"I am not a mechanic," Leif said in an offended voice.
"But I do know there are many things one can do to an
engine to make sure it will not start."

"They can't have done anything drastic," I argued.
"This must be the craft they plan to use when they leave."

"Unless they have arranged for a boat or helicopter to
pick them up," Leif said.

I hadn't thought of that. It didn't make me feel very
good.

"In any case, it would take hours to check the cruiser,"
Leif said. "The ignition system, the fuel lines, and so on.
Do you suppose Max will stand back and allow us to do
that?"

"How did you get here?" I asked.

Leif blinked. "I swam."

Through the open doors I could see the distant shore
and the waves that rose and fell in brisk cadence. The
water was a deep, rich blue; it looked as cold as a freezer.
No wonder Leif's calf muscles looked like the hawsers of
the *Q.E. II.*

"What about your brother?"

"You don't give up, do you?" Leif said admiringly.

"I can't imagine him swimming."

"No." Leif's face lengthened. "I did not ask how he came. Possibly he hired someone to bring him across. What is the use of this, Vicky? There is no boat we can use."

"I have to agree with that." Hands in my pockets, I went out onto the dock. Leif followed.

"I believe your fears are needless," he said. "The man, Max, means you no harm. Let him have his gold. What value does it have?"

"I don't give a damn about the treasure," I said, not quite truthfully. "But I'm not stupid enough to trust Max's word. Besides, I can't turn my back on deliberate, cold-blooded murder."

"Smythe deserves it," Leif said.

I turned away. He grabbed my wrist and spun me around to face him. His eyes glittered like topaz.

"You think I am cruel, like those criminals? No, no. When you hear you will understand why I do not risk my life, or yours, to save such vermin."

I knew I had to hear it sooner or later, and I despised myself for being so reluctant to learn the truth. "All right, all right," I said resignedly. "Let's go up and sit in the garden. If I have to listen to a rotten story, I might as well have something pretty to look at."

It was as rotten a story as I could have imagined. Even the scent of the flowers didn't lessen the sickness that mounted as I heard what Leif had to say.

"He is only twenty-six. You would not think it to see him, would you? Even as a child he was brilliant, a genius. He won his doctorate from your Harvard University and was appointed to the dig at Tiryns in Greece. You read, perhaps, of the discovery of the royal tombs?"

Naturally I had; it had been the archaeological sensation of the year. So that was why Georg Hasseltine's name was familiar to me.

"It could have been the making of his career," Leif said somberly. "Instead it was the end of him. By accident the director discovered that one of the treasures—a golden mask, like the ones found at Mycenae—was a clever fake. Georg had stolen and sold the original. You can guess to whom he sold it."

Even if I had not known, I would have recognized John's fine Italian hand. He didn't go in for blatant breaking and entering. Half the museums in Europe owned fraudulent pieces, left by John in place of the originals he had made off with. I don't know what perverse instinct made me try to defend him.

"Your brother could have refused his offer," I said.

"He was only a boy! And there was a woman—someone Smythe had supplied, I do not doubt, along with the deadly white powder to which Georg is now a slave. . . . You know the man's power over the innocent. He ruined Georg. There was no scandal—universities do not love publicity—but the word was passed. No one would employ him. In despair he turned to petty crime. Whenever I found him and tried to help, he eluded me. And always he has searched for Smythe, to take revenge. I followed him across half the world. Not to help him kill, as you think—no. I would not weep to see that man destroyed, but I could not let my brother commit murder."

I patted his arm sympathetically. Georg was a weak fool, who had traded an honorable career for quick profit, but that didn't excuse what John had done.

"And now he has fallen again." With a groan Leif buried his head in his hands. "Helping these criminals to rob . . ."

"Maybe he's only pretending to cooperate—gaining Max's confidence in order to double-cross him."

The phrase was not well chosen. Leif shook his head despairingly. "I wish I could believe it. But I dare not. Do not trust him, Vicky. Tell him nothing of your plans."

I was relieved I hadn't had to make that point myself. "I won't, Leif."

"You have plans?" He studied me keenly, then smiled. "Yes, you do. You are stubborn. You don't give in. What is a man to do with such a woman?"

"Just don't get in my way, Leif."

"I would be afraid!" His eyes widened in pretended terror.

I had to admire his resilience—from tragedy to corny jokes in the space of a few seconds. "So," he said, "if you are determined, I must help you. What shall we do?"

"The first thing is to find Gus."

"How?"

"I think he's here, on the island." I explained why I thought so. Leif nodded.

"It is reasonable. But if you are wrong?"

"Then I'm wrong. But what's the harm in looking? We can't make a move until Gus is free."

"What kind of move?" He put his arm around me.

I pulled away. "Not now, Leif. I'm not in the mood."

"Rest and be still for a moment," Leif said softly. "You are forcing yourself beyond your strength. Your heart is pounding."

He had cause to know. I tried to relax. Even my teeth were clenched.

The wind stitched the water into little white ruffles, and a flock of fleecy clouds glided serenely across the sky.

Above the emerald hills snowcapped mountains shone in the sun.

"It's no use," I said, wriggling out from Leif's embrace. "I can't relax, I can't sit still, and I don't want you to pat me and ask stupid questions. I want you to *do* something."

"I will do whatever you want. Only tell me."

"I'm trying to think. With the boats out of commission, there's no way of getting off the island. Maybe you could swim to shore; maybe I could. But I doubt that Gus is able, not with that leg of his."

"That is right. I have a plan."

"Yes?" I turned hopefully.

"We find the old man." Leif tossed this off as if it were a matter of locating a pair of misplaced spectacles. "Then you take him to a hiding place. In the trees, or—or somewhere. I will swim the lake and go for help."

"What about your brother?"

Leif didn't answer immediately. Lips pressed tightly together, forehead furrowed, he appeared to be wrestling with thoughts too painful for utterance. Finally he said, "I will take care of Georg. But, Vicky—tell him nothing. Tell Smythe nothing. We can trust no one except our two selves."

ii

Much as I hate having the narrative interrupted by long paragraphs of description, I guess I had better give you some idea of the terrain, since it figures prominently in succeeding events. As I said, the shape of the island was roughly triangular, the sides longer than the base, and the end blunted. The house was located on this blunt end. Behind the house the land rose, culminating in a plateau of rough pasture that formed the central portion of the island. The western side of the triangle was heavily wooded, in a belt that curved northward and expanded to fill the base of the triangle. On the east the land sloped down to the water, ending in a boggy section of swamp-land.

Searching for Gus, and for any other useful piece of information we might encounter, Leif and I followed a graveled path that circled the house. Behind the main building lay a group of sheds and stables, a big beautiful stone barn, and, in their own hedged enclosure, several small cottages that had probably housed servants in the days when the main house was fully staffed. Though their tiny yards were free of weeds, and their windows shone cleanly, they appeared to be unoccupied—even by a prisoner.

As we approached the barn, a man stepped out from behind its wall. He had the swarthy, brachycephalic look of a southern Italian or Sicilian, but I was unable to confirm this identification by his speech, since he said not a word. He simply showed us his rifle. We took the hint.

"Could Gus be in one of those sheds?" I asked, when we were out of earshot.

"More likely the man is guarding tools that we might use as weapons."

Our path led through a gate in a high stone wall, into a grove of trees. Unlike the natural woodland that fringed much of the island, these giant firs appeared to have been planted as a windbreak. They were well tended, and the ground was free of underbrush. The breeze murmured in the high branches; the sound of our footsteps was deadened by a thick layer of fallen needles.

Coming out of the trees, we climbed a steep slope and found ourselves on the plateau. In the middle of the pasture I saw a group of men—or, to put it more accurately, the torsos of a group of men. The high grass hid the lower parts of their bodies.

At one time the pasture had been cultivated. Nobody had plowed it recently, though. It had been allowed to revert to grass, weeds, and wild flowers. The growth seemed unusually luxuriant for the climate and the season. Perhaps Gus's grandpa's experiments had involved a lavish use of fertilizer.

Leif pushed gallantly ahead, trampling down the grass and muttering about snakes. I doubted there were any, but I stored the idea away for purposes of harassment. City slickers, who take muggers, traffic, and pollution for granted, tend to panic when faced with rural perils.

Never had I seen so obvious a collection of urbanites. Georg was the only one who wasn't staring uneasily at the wide-open spaces. The false euphoria of the drug he used was at its peak; he was talking animatedly, punctuating his speech with expansive gestures. As we drew closer I heard him say:

"It will take at least a month. With only six men, and no proper tools—perhaps longer. Surely you must have more specific information."

Max must have seen us—singly, Leif and I were hard to miss, and as a pair we were outstanding—but since he paid me no attention, I saw no reason why I should favor him with a "Good morning." I sat down on a boulder and watched with malicious pleasure as Max helplessly surveyed the sea of grass stretching out all around. If you have ever tried to dig a garden—a moderate-sized plot, thirty feet on a side—you can understand the little man's distress.

"The pasture behind the house," he said finally. "That is all I know."

"But you have nothing!" Georg waved his arms. "Not the most rudimentary equipment for a dig."

Max indicated a wheelbarrow. "Picks, shovels, hoes—"

"And a metal detector." Georg lifted the instrument off the wheelbarrow and sneered at it. "Excellent for finding tin cans on beaches. Hopeless for your purpose. Now if you had brought a proton magnetometer, or an electrical resistivity instrument . . ."

"I can get them," Max said eagerly. "I will send Hans—"

"No use." Georg waved the offer aside. "Oh, perhaps if the circumstances were different . . . But you have no trained personnel. I cannot do everything myself."

Max's eyes wandered in my direction. I waved a casual hand. "Count me out, Max. I'm no archaeologist. I wouldn't know a proton whatchamacallit from a toaster."

"Also," Georg went on, "in such a stony soil, and an area of heavy rainfall . . ."

Max gritted his teeth. "How long would such a survey take, with these instruments?"

"Hmmm." Georg fondled his beard. "We would need a source of electricity, naturally. The probes of the resistivity meter should be placed no more than one meter apart—"

A bleat of fury came from Max. "One meter? Do you know the size of this field?"

"About three acres, I would suppose," was the calm reply.

"We dig," Max said shortly. "All of us."

"Very well," Georg said. "First we must mow the field."

It would take too long and serve no useful purpose to report Max's comments. Eventually one of the men was sent to the house to fetch scythes, and the work began.

Leif wandered off, perhaps fearing that Max would put him to work. He needn't have worried; Max wasn't naive enough to put a large cutting instrument into Leif's hands. He missed a treat. Watching those inept goons trying to cut grass made my morning. Nobody got decapitated, but Pierre almost lost his left foot to a wild swipe from Hans.

When the slapstick palled, I got up and strolled around, giving the mowers a wide berth. To the northwest, almost hidden by the trees, I caught a glimpse of what appeared to be the roof of a building. When I sauntered to that side of the pasture, a sharp command from Max sent one of the boys after me, waving his gun. So I went back to my rock.

Toward midday John appeared, picking a delicate path through the weeds. His attire was country-casual: old tweeds, a cashmere sweater, and a tie with the insignia of some institution—possibly Sing-Sing or Wormwood Scrubbs.

After a leisurely survey of the proceedings he joined me on my rock, dusting off the surface with an immaculate handkerchief before planting his tailored bottom on it.

I rose ostentatiously, and he said, "Now, now, this is no time for petty spite. We ought to have a little chat about . . ." Max trotted toward us and John went on, without a change of tone, ". . . lunch. Who's in charge of the kitchen?"

"A good question," Max said.

"I suppose you all expect me to do it," I grumbled.

"You object?" Max inquired.

"Of course I object. But I guess I haven't much choice."

Before Max could comment, John said quickly, "I wouldn't advise it, Max. When a liberated woman offers to take on a chore that violates her precious principles, she always has an ulterior motive."

"I do not underrate Dr. Bliss's intelligence," Max said. "We can subsist on cold meats and cheese for a few days."

He gave me a patronizing smile. I said, addressing the air six inches above John's head, "You lousy fink."

"It was a rather ingenuous attempt," John said. "Max is not ingenuous."

"No," Max agreed. "Nor am I stupid enough to permit the two of you to confer privately. Smythe, since you are so concerned about your stomach, I will put you in charge. Bring the food here. We will have a luncheon al fresco—a picnic, as you would say."

"What makes you think he won't poison you?" I asked. "His motive is more pressing than mine."

"I am glad you realize that." Max bowed. "He will not poison the food because Pierre will watch every move he makes. Nothing elaborate, Smythe—bread, cheese, ham, beer. And don't forget a bottle opener."

Pierre was happy to be reassigned. His cohorts looked at him enviously as they mopped their dripping faces. Grass speckled them like green freckles. Hans complained that he was getting a blister on his thumb.

I might have known John would make a production out of the simple task. He and Pierre came back loaded with baskets and boxes, not to mention cushions and rugs and other luxuries. Among the latter was a stringed instrument of some variety—it looked like a cross between a lute and a guitar—that John had slung over his shoulder by its elaborately woven strap. Max's eyebrows rose when he saw this device, but he did not comment.

It was—to put it mildly—an unusual kind of picnic. Sprawled on the rough ground munching sandwiches, we were not exactly your normal little gathering of friends. The assorted artillery struck a particularly inappropriate note. Max was the only one of the gang who wasn't visibly armed to the teeth, but when he leaned forward to reach for a beer I saw the butt of an automatic under his coat. Other than that he didn't look out of place. It was only my awareness of what he really was that gave his face a sinister cast. Before I knew his identity I had thought him inoffensive and harmless-looking.

The same could not be said of the others. Except for Hans, whose blunt features had the deceptive innocence of vacuity, the faces bore the same stamp of evil. There were six of them—Max and Hans and Pierre, a sandy-haired character who spoke German with a thick Austrian accent, another Frenchman, and a dapper little man with the coldest eyes I have ever seen. His name was Rudi, and he appeared to be an eastern European, country unknown but probably glad to be rid of Rudi. The (presumed) Italian guarding the barn made seven, but I couldn't be sure that was the complete contingent.

After lunch Pierre took the empty bottles back to the house and the dig began in earnest. John reclined on his cushions like a sultan watching the serfs at work and strummed his guitar. I knew he played the piano with considerable skill, but I had not realized his musical talents were so diversified. He sang one folk song after another, in a dozen different languages; from time to time he switched to a piercing falsetto. If I hadn't been so furious with him, I'd have enjoyed the game. It reduced poor old Max to the brink of hysteria. Every time he looked at John resting and crooning, he got a shade redder.

Leif, who had returned when the food appeared, sat like a monolith, hands on his bent knees, eyes fixed on his brother. Georg had found some stakes and string and was setting up a grid system, like any normal archaeologist preparing a normal excavation. There was something terrifying about his intense absorption. It was as if he were living in a world totally removed from the realm the rest of us inhabited—a world of crime and kidnapping and mass murder.

The crooks dug. Max clung stubbornly to his metal detector; whenever he located something the gang flew into action. By late afternoon they had dug up a horseshoe, a rusty ax blade, and seven tin cans. John was asleep, his lute across his knees; Leif was still brooding; and I was bored to screaming point.

"I'm halfway tempted to help dig," I said to Leif.

"What?" He turned drowsy eyes toward me.

"Wake up, dammit. We've got to do something; we can't just sit here."

"What?" It was a different kind of "what." At least he was paying attention.

"Well . . . plan. Have you had any new ideas?"

"The old man is not in the house," Leif said. "There was a shortwave radio. It is smashed."

"I think I know where Gus is being held. Look over there."

Leif caught my hand as I raised it to point. "He will hear you," he muttered, nodding at John.

"He's asleep."

"He is not."

John opened one eye. "If either of you has a useful idea, I wish you'd let me in on it. No one can possibly be more interested than I in finding a way out of this."

"Cheer up," I said heartlessly. "Max and the boys will be too tired to torture you tonight."

"They are torturing him now," Leif said, in a tone as flat and hard as the rock against which he leaned. "Waiting for the inevitable is the most painful torment of all. Never knowing at what moment the executioner's sword will descend . . ." He made a graphic, shocking gesture, drawing his hand across his throat and opening his mouth in a silent scream.

Seeing my expression, he smiled apologetically. "I ask your pardon. I do not care for this man. If I were not civilized, I would help Max to kill him."

"But you are civilized," I pointed out. "We may as well join forces, since we're all in the same boat. Keeping in mind," and I turned a critical eye toward John, "that we can't trust the dirty dog an inch unless his self-interest is involved."

"My self-interest is deeply involved in my own survival," John said sincerely. "And my best hope of survival is with you. I'd gladly cooperate with Max, but he won't let me."

"What have you to contribute to the general welfare?" I asked.

"The first thing, as our Leif has so brilliantly suggested, is to find Gus. That hut in the trees is a definite possibility. Someone ought to check it out."

"Someone?" I said.

"You've the best chance of moving about unobserved. Max likes you. Whatever did you do to win his heart?"

"Mom always told me that good manners and consideration for the feelings of others paid off in the end," I said.

"That's always been my motto as well; but it doesn't seem to be working at present. No matter; Max has a soft spot for you. And he has the typical middle-aged European male tendency to underestimate women."

"You can eliminate two of those adjectives," I said.

"I don't underestimate you," John assured me, with a flash of blue eyes. "However, I'll volunteer for the job. Any distraction you could provide would be gratefully received."

"What sort of distraction did you have in mind?"

"Improvise, love, improvise. We can't make plans until we know what security measures Max has in mind for tonight."

"Hmph." I turned to Leif, who had withdrawn into his private thoughts, and jabbed his elbow. "What do you think, Leif?"

"I am wondering," Leif said, "how much longer it will be before Max decides the project is hopeless."

Chapter Seven

I HAD BEEN wondering the same thing. Both men relapsed into moody silence. Leif's unblinking stare settled on John, and the latter began to show signs of strain. His face remained studiedly bland, but when he picked up the guitar he produced a series of chords so consistently off key that I suspect his fingers were none too steady.

I wandered toward the end of the field where the men were working. Georg was puttering away in his own little section. He had removed the topsoil from an area about a meter square. It was an academically neat excavation, with sharp right-angle corners and a level surface; at that rate it would take him about ten years to cover the entire field.

Max's haphazard digging was no more impressive. The areas of exposed subsoil looked pitifully small amid the rolling waves of stubble. It *was* a hopeless project; a whole crew working for three months might accomplish something. Might . . . Nobody knew how deep the treasure was buried, or how widely it was scattered—or even if it was there.

Max stood with his shoulders bowed as he watched the diggers. "Can I go back to the house?" I asked meekly. "I'm bored."

"If you like." He didn't look at me. I took that for a bad sign. As I turned away he added, "We will all be returning shortly." And that was an even worse sign.

The sun was high and surprisingly hot. I headed for the shower. The cool water streaming over my body improved my physical state, but mentally I was in a grim mood. Max and his men, who had been engaging in strenuous physical activity most of the day, would be even hotter and dirtier and more discouraged than I. If Max had had any archaeological experience he would have seen at first glance that he couldn't hope to find what he was looking for in the space of a few days. Sitting in his city office, he had probably visualized the procedure with the mental eye of ignorant optimism—a stretch of dirt about twenty feet square, with bits of gold sticking up out of the soil. He might be ignorant, but he wasn't stupid, nor was he the man to waste time on a hopeless project.

I cut my shower short. I wanted to search the house before they got back.

Max and his crew had taken over one wing, the one on the south, corresponding to the flanking wing in which my bedroom was located. All the doors along the corridor were locked. I figured there wasn't any point in trying to pick the locks. Max was not the man to leave weapons, or any other useful item, lying around.

On the second floor were more bedrooms, none of them in use. The curtains were drawn, the furniture draped with white dustcloths. One chamber, larger than the rest, with an adjoining bath and dressing room, was fancy enough to have been the master's quarters. Perhaps Gus had occupied it until his physical handicap made stairs difficult. I opened the door of one of the heavy oak wardrobes. It was filled with women's dresses, swathed in linen to keep off the dust. A strong smell of mothballs wafted out—the odor of the past, of memories preserved and cherished. . . . Feeling like an intruder, I tiptoed out.

A door under the stairs presumably led to the cellar. It was locked and looked heavy enough to withstand a battering ram. I pressed my ear against it and then ventured a soft "Gus? Are you there?" If he was, he didn't answer.

I had explored the whole house except for one area— the kitchen and service section. It lay behind the dining room, separated from the latter by a butler's pantry whose shelves were filled with shining glassware.

When I walked into the kitchen my first thought was, "Poor Mrs. Andersson." So far the mess wasn't too bad— dusty footprints dulling the white stone floor, trays of dirty coffee cups and dishes put down anywhere on counters and tables. But it was bound to get worse before it got better, and I could see that this was the housekeeper's favorite place—sitting room as well as workshop. One end of the big room had been furnished with woven rugs, rocking chairs, and a few tables. An enormous peasant-style pewter cupboard stood against the wall, its looming blue sides painted with bright pink roses and red hearts. In the cupboard section, under the open shelves, were some of Mrs. Andersson's personal belongings, including stacks of magazines and a knitting bag. The latter held balls of soft gray yarn and one sleeve of a man's sweater, almost completed. If she was a confirmed knitter, like some of my aunts, she probably worked on several projects simultaneously; this was the one she picked up when she sat rocking, after the meal had been served and the maids were cleaning the kitchen. I could see her sitting there, swaying back and forth in time with the click of her needles, her face calm. . . . Suddenly the unwashed dishes and dusty floor struck me as horrible and disgusting.

Blue-and-white-checked curtains swayed at the windows, and sunlight streaked the flagstone floor. Except for a few homey touches of that nature, the working end of the kitchen was a model of modern efficiency, and every appliance was the best procurable—refrigerator, stove, two wall ovens, and a couple of kilometers of counter space and cupboards.

I started opening cupboard doors. Mrs. Andersson might be a traditional, old-fashioned lady, but she had a sneaking fascination for the latest in cooking gadgets. I had never seen such things, except in gourmet-kitchen shops—the latest-model Cuisinart, with every attachment known to man or woman, an electric pasta maker, an ice-cream machine—not the Italian model with which I was familiar, which retails at a mere four hundred dollars, but the aristocrat of ice-cream makers, a Minigel. There were an American milkshake mixer, a German coffeemaker with a built-in digital clock timer, a Danish waffle iron. . . .

I was raised by a Swedish cook—two of them, in fact, for when my grandmother came to visit, she kicked Mom out of the kitchen and took over. Being a normal child, I had fought the efforts of these ladies to turn me into another of the same breed, but they had molded me better than they, or I, had realized. Mrs. Andersson's kitchen brought old instincts to reluctant life.

Drawers and more cupboards. . . . Baking pans of every variety, for quiches, for tarts, for *madeleines,* for popovers.

Molds for plum pudding and shortbread. Rosette irons, woks, fish poachers, larding skewers, artichoke steamers, poachette rings. . . . What the poor, frustrated woman did with all of it I could not imagine. If Gus was as antisocial as he claimed, she didn't often get the chance to cook an elaborate meal. Maybe she played with her toys during the long winter evenings and stuffed the housemaid and the gardener with chocolate shakes, poached eggs, and apricot flan.

As I continued to explore, I saw there was one conspicuous omission in the collection. No knives, no cleavers, nothing with a sharp edge. The knife we had used at lunch was on the table, its surface dulled by smears of cheese and sausage. The message was as clear as print: Don't try it—my absence will be duly noted. Besides, it was a foot and a half long, not the sort of weapon a girl can conceal in her bra.

Next to the kitchen was a pantry, its shelves filled with canned and packaged and bottled goods. A deep freeze muttered and clicked in one corner. We wouldn't starve, at any rate. No, we wouldn't starve. . . .

The deep freeze was packed to the brim. Thoughtfully I hefted a ten-pound roast, and those suppressed impulses stirred anew. They weren't violent impulses—I was not contemplating a murderous assault on Max with a frozen rump roast. I didn't need to resort to esoteric blunt instruments; the house and grounds abounded in large, hard, lumpy objects. I had no intention of getting that close to Max or any of his boys.

I put the roast back into the freezer and opened the fridge. The signs of clumsy foraging were only too evident; the food was all jumbled around, and some oaf had tipped over a jar of jam, which had leaked over two shelves before forming a sticky puddle on the bottom.

Ancestral urges won. I cleaned up the mess. When I
started to straighten the shelves, the first thing I found
was a large fish. The layers of plastic wrap encasing it did
not dull the hostile gleam of its bulging eyes. Pikes are not
your ordinary placid fish—they are predators, and look as
mean as they act.

The fish had been cleaned and scaled, and the gills
removed, so I assumed it was supposed to be served with
the head intact. I had never eaten pike, but my grandmother used to bake trout that way, brushed with beaten
egg and sprinkled with bread crumbs.

Well, why not? I had nothing better to do at the moment.

A short time later the place was—not spotless, I'll never
be a good Swedish housewife. But it was clean. The dishes
were washed and stacked, the floor was swept, and attractive smells were seeping out of the saucepans that bub-
bled on the stove. The pike was in one of the ovens, sans
its head. Mrs. Andersson and Granny wouldn't have ap-
proved of decapitation, but I can't stand those boiled
white eyes looking up at me from a plate. When I opened
the other oven, a heavenly odor almost canceled out the
stench of fish. The freezer had contained stacks of pies,
tarts, and pastries. All had been neatly labeled, but since
my Swedish is minimal, the labels were of no use to me.
This pie looked, and smelled, like red raspberry.

The first to respond to the smell of cooking was the cat.
I had been wondering where it was; that cozy little sitting
area absolutely demanded a fat, purring cat. It came in
through the window, startling me so that I dropped the
spoon I held—a big, fluffy tabby, its forehead marked
with the customary black M, its jowls outlined in white.
Tail elevated and bristling, it studied me warily for a
moment, and I stared back, mesmerized by its glowing

green eyes. Then it opened its mouth and emitted a lady-like, dainty little mew.

While the cat wove in and out around my feet, purring hoarsely, I found its bowl in a cupboard, and a can of cat food, identifiable by the picture on the label, in the pantry. He (his sex was obvious, as soon as he turned his back) tucked into the food with that accusing air of imminent starvation typical of cats. I wasn't too worried about him. The island probably abounded in small rodents, and he had already demonstrated a commendable caution in approaching strangers. His chances of survival were probably better than mine.

When the kitchen door opened, he scuttled for cover under the table. He didn't move fast enough.

"What a touching tableau," John exclaimed. "The cook and her cat. Hello, cat." He squatted.

After a moment a suspicious whiskered face appeared. The two of them contemplated one another in solemn silence for a time. Then, with a kind of feline shrug, the cat gave John an unmistakable cold shoulder and returned to its dinner.

"Crushed again," said John. Rising, he sniffed appreciatively. "What's for dinner?"

"Your dinner? I haven't the faintest idea."

John raised one eyebrow—a trick of his I particularly abhor—and wandered into the pantry. I lifted the lid of a skillet. Whole onions, cooked in butter and brown sugar, simmered in half a cup of beef stock. John came back empty-handed but unperturbed. Whistling, he opened the refrigerator door and draped himself over it, staring into the fridge in that maddening way men and children have, as if they expected a seven-course meal to materialize on a shelf. I almost snapped, "Close that door." I must have heard Mother say it a thousand times.

To my chagrin John found the food I had pushed to the back of the shelves. I suppose Mrs. Andersson had taken it out of the freezer the night before. Murmuring affectionately, he removed a bowl of kidneys, a box of mushrooms, and the butter.

"Lend me the knife," he said abstractedly.

I borrowed it back a little later to slice cabbage. John stirred things into his sautéed kidneys and mushrooms and fed scraps to the cat. It had transferred its fickle affections to John, and ignored me completely. Obviously it preferred kidney to canned food.

It went out the window in a long, flowing leap when the others started to file in. They stood around watching and sniffing hopefully. I drained my potatoes and put them through the ricer, added butter and a generous amount of hot milk. John tossed linguine into a big pot of boiling water. Everybody else drooled.

Leif was the last to appear. He had showered and changed, and he looked like the kind of man a wife hopes will come home for dinner. I gave him a melting smile and waved my spoon toward the rocking chairs. "Sit down, Leif. Supper will be ready in a few minutes."

With a broadening grin he took in the two chairs, the table with two place settings, and the ring of hungry faces. "I will get us something to drink," he said.

I suggested a light Riesling, to go with the fish, and told him where to find it in the pantry. As he opened the bottle, I met Max's narrowed eyes.

"I'm sure you wouldn't trust anything I cooked," I said guilelessly.

"I have enough for everyone," John announced, sloshing his linguine into a colander. Max turned his hostile stare onto John, who said impatiently, "I don't give a damn whether you eat it or not, Max, but it surely must have occurred to you, as it has to Dr. Bliss, that poisoning is an extremely slow and chancy method of incapacitating a large-sized group."

Max thought this over, and as the truth of it dawned, his cheeks turned the color of fresh liver. "But you were the one," he began.

"I just threw that idea out to liven things up," John said. "Have a kidney."

The pike was delicious. I guess the kidneys were too. The gang polished them off and gobbled up everything else in sight, including the remains of the pike, which I magnanimously contributed. Fish is no good the second day anyway.

"Oh, dear," John said, surveying the scraped plates. "I ought to have made meatballs too. Never mind, we'll have them tomorrow night."

This hopeful suggestion hung twitching and dying in midair like a hooked fish. Max grunted and pushed his chair from the table.

"Oh, no, you don't," I said, as the rest followed suit. "I cleaned up one mess today. It's your turn for KP."

I honestly didn't expect this order would be obeyed, but after a moment Max nodded. "Sir John will oblige."

"Sir John" looked mutinous. "It's not fair. I did the cooking."

For a minute it appeared the situation was going to develop into one of those all too familiar family squabbles, like the ones my brothers and I had every day of our lives. "It's your turn tonight. No, it's not, I did it yesterday. You did not, I traded with you Tuesday. . . ."

Max banged his fist on the table. "Hans."

"Aber, Herr Max, ich weiss nicht—"

I decided to get out and leave them to settle it. The argument broke out again as soon as I left the room.

Somehow I was not surprised to see that John had also slipped out.

"Shall we take a little stroll in the garden?" he asked.

"That's what I had in mind. A solitary stroll."

Trotting to keep up with me, he remarked, "I sense a specific source of annoyance, over and above the general vexation I seem to arouse in you. You'd better tell me what it is; we can't work efficiently while you are nursing some fancied grudge."

I spun around. He ground to a halt and ducked, just in time to avoid the fist I shook under his nose. "Annoyance? I never had a very exaggerated opinion of your morals, but after seeing the end product of your latest caper I am not inclined to add myself to the list of victims."

"Ah—Georg."

"Georg," I agreed.

"I suppose you wouldn't believe me if I told you I was not responsible."

"I wouldn't."

"We'd all have a better chance of getting out of this if you could bring yourself to cooperate with me."

"You cooperate first," I said.

"If I'm to get out of the house tonight, I'll need your help." He broke off with a grunt of exasperation as the front door opened and Rudi appeared. "Pretend to be angry," he muttered.

"No trouble." I slapped his face hard. He yelled. Rudi grinned—at least I think the slit in the lower part of his face was intended to be a smile.

John retreated into the house, ostentatiously nursing his cheek. Rudi followed. I went down the steps into the garden.

The roses were beginning to bloom. I touched a creamy

bud; its opening petals were as translucent as fine porcelain. Gus had talked about his rose garden the night before. His mother had set it out, nursing the prize plants through the long cold winter. Gus was enormously proud of it.

Where was he now, the kind old man who had welcomed kin so warmly? If he met his death through my carelessness and lack of foresight I would never forgive myself.

It was still bright daylight, and would be for many hours. If John meant to prowl tonight, he wouldn't have a long period of darkness at his disposal. In fact, he might not have any. This far north, with midsummer almost upon us, a deep dusk is the most one can expect in the way of night. John would need all the distraction he could get, there was no question about that.

In the crystal-clear air the distant mountains of Norway looked like a low-hanging white cloud, the snow on their peaks shimmering in reflected sunlight. The lake was as calm as a fish pond. The island was almost in the center of the lake, but the distance between our dock and the one opposite, on the mainland, seemed slightly shorter than it was elsewhere. If we had to swim, that was the obvious route—straight toward the garage-boathouse on shore. Gus was the one I was worried about; but with Leif to help, I could probably get him across. If we could get even fifteen minutes' start, night or day . . . Surely there would be people at the boathouse during the day, villagers who kept their boats there, and the old codgers. A flash of light caught my eye. It came from the shadows under the eaves of the garage, and as I squinted, shading my eyes with my hand, I thought I saw them—five shapes, rigid as statues in their wooden chairs.

"Laugh," said a voice behind me.

I turned with a start. "Laugh," Max repeated, taking my arm. "One of them is watching us through binoculars."

I stretched my mouth into a gaping grin. The crown of his dead, flat gray hair barely reached my nose, but the pressure of his fingers bit into my bicep. I let him turn me toward the house.

"They are only inquisitive old men, with nothing better to do," Max went on. "But I would not want you to succumb to a foolish impulse. The situation has not changed. Mr. Jonsson is still in my hands, and if a signal from you brought one of those doddering ancients to the rescue, he would only be added to my collection of hostages."

"I have only your word for it that Gus is still alive," I said, as he opened the door for me.

"I wondered when you would bring that up. Would you like to talk to him?"

He led the way into the study. I took a chair by the desk while he opened a cupboard and removed a canvas-wrapped bundle. He made no attempt to conceal what he was doing. I suppose he thought I wouldn't have enough technical knowledge to recognize the device.

I hadn't seen that particular model before—it was a good deal more sophisticated than the ones my brothers had owned—but I recognized it as a kind of wireless walkie-talkie. Max pushed a few buttons, and a long antenna wavered out. He pressed more buttons.

A harsh voice croaked a few words. Max answered in English, obviously the lingua franca of that cosmopolitan group. "Put Mr. Jonsson on."

After an interval I heard Gus's voice. "Vicky? Are you there, my dear?"

"Gus! Gus, are you okay?"

"Yes, they have not hurt me. Have they hurt you?"

"No. Don't worry about me, Gus, I'm fine."

"Do nothing, Vicky. Do what they say. Take no risk."

Before I could answer, Max played a tattoo on the buttons and the antenna retracted. He returned the gadget to the cupboard, locked it, and tucked the key ostentatiously into his jacket pocket.

He needn't have worried. The walkie-talkie wouldn't do me any good; it obviously had a limited range. I had been right all along—Gus was on the island. And now I knew where on the island.

I suspected the conversation had been set up in order to calm Gus as well as me. The hostage situation worked both ways; he wouldn't try anything while I was in Max's hands. At least I hoped to God he wouldn't. He was a proud man, unaccustomed to intimidation, and if he lost his temper he might do something rash. The sooner I put my half-baked plan into action, the better. I had to cooperate with John. I knew it, and he knew it too. He had the best chance of scouting unseen; he could move like a shadow, and he knew dirty tricks I had never heard of. I figured I could count on him not to double-cross me, because he needed me as much as I needed him. Alone he was no match for Max and the boys, especially since Leif and Georg weren't too crazy about him either.

My meditations were interrupted by an object that came flying in through the open window. It landed on a table and squatted there, staring with malevolent emerald eyes.

"Ah," Max exclaimed. "What a beautiful cat. Hello, my friend; what is your name?" He held out his hand and made cooing sounds.

To my surprise and disgust, the cat promptly responded. Another flying leap took it to the desk. Max scratched it under the chin. Not only did it accept the caress, it squirmed and wriggled and started to purr.

"So much," I said, "for stereotypes."

Leif would have said, "What?" Max laughed, his hand moving over the cat's head and neck with practiced skill.

"I'm sorry to disturb your prejudices, Dr. Bliss. I am very fond of animals, and they like me. I have a cat of my own, an aristocratic Siamese named Marguerite."

He certainly knew how to handle the species. The big tabby literally drooled on him. Finally it flung itself on its back in an abandonment of bliss, knocking Max's brief-case to the floor. The crash startled it. With a hiss it bounced up and departed, via the window.

Smiling, Max bent to pick up his possessions. The briefcase had sprung open, scattering the contents—scissors, black papers, white cardboard mounts. Not all the papers were black, however. A few sheets were scarlet, bright as fresh blood.

"You use red paper?" I asked curiously.

Max's deft hands paused in their work of gathering up the papers. "Sometimes," he said curtly.

"When the mood takes you, or . . ." The funniest feeling came over me; I don't know why. I swallowed. "Or—or for a particular reason?"

"For a particular . . . collection." Max straightened, the briefcase in his hands. His eyes avoided mine. "We all have personal idiosyncrasies, Dr. Bliss."

"Right," I mumbled. "Sure."

Max selected a sheet of black paper. "You permit?"

I gave him the profile he wanted, without further comment. He made a sound of satisfaction. "You are a good subject, Dr. Bliss. Such well-defined features."

The sticky subject had been dropped. We were back on our old terms. I thought I knew the significance of the scarlet silhouettes, and I was no more anxious to talk about them than Max was. But, my God, the psychological impact of that little "idiosyncrasy" . . .

Max was still snipping when a delegation trooped in, headed by John. He gestured at Rudi.

"Must I have Peter Lorre dogging my footsteps?"

Instead of appearing offended, Rudi beamed with pleasure. I suppose if you are imitating a villain, it is a compliment to be compared to one of the greatest.

"I have decided you require a permanent escort," Max said equably. "Don't feel persecuted; Mr. Hasseltine will also be guarded."

He indicated Hans. That literal-minded soul was standing so close to Leif that his heavy breathing blew the latter's hair into his face. Leif glowered.

"I will not endure this," he exclaimed.

"Sit down!" Max shouted. "All of you, sit and be quiet. I am in no mood for childishness tonight."

I gestured toward the sofa where I was sitting, and Leif joined me. Hans tried to squeeze his bulk into the narrow space between us. "Hey," I said. Max rolled his eyes.

"Heaven give me patience. Hans, take a chair—that one, behind the sofa."

Everyone subsided. The glum silence was broken by Max. He held up the finished silhouette.

"It is not so pleasant as the last," he said in a worried voice.

"I don't feel as pleasant," I assured him. He had caught my scowl and out-thrust lip quite accurately.

Max picked up another piece of paper. It was black, not scarlet, but as his eyes focused on John, the latter sprang from his chair as if he had been stung.

"This is a dull group," he announced. "What about a game?"

Without waiting for an answer, he threw open one of

the cupboard doors. "Chess, checkers, Go, Monopoly. . . .
He must have bought out a toy shop. Anyone for a game
of Scrabble?"

"Why not?" I stood up.

I don't know what John would have done if someone
else had accepted his offer. In fact, I didn't know what he
was going to do now that I had accepted it. The maneuver
was pretty obvious. Max thought so too. His eyes spar-
kled with malicious amusement.

"What a charming idea. We will all be entertained.
Rudi, sit at the table and call out the words as they are
played."

Apparently undisturbed by this suggestion, John
poured the tiles out onto the table. I helped him turn them
over and watched approvingly as he gave them a very
perfunctory shuffle. I palmed the pieces I wanted—not
very expertly, but nobody saw me. All eyes were glued on
John.

I moved first. That was fine with me. I had only one
question, but it was an important question, and I wasn't
sure when, if ever, I would have an opportunity to talk
privately with John.

I spelled out "boss" and rolled my eyes in Max's direction as Rudi intoned the word like a bingo announcer.

"No, no," John said. There was a brief but perceptible
pause before he added, "You'll have to do better than
that, my girl."

The confirmation came as no surprise. Directors of big
criminal organizations don't go into the field; they sit in
fancy offices in New York or Hamburg or Marseilles, and
give generous donations to charity. I realized there was
another question I needed to ask, and cheated shamelessly
as I collected my next tiles. Rudi didn't notice; he was
watching John.

John spelled "distract," using the second *s* in "boss," then folded his hands and smiled at me. One thumb was folded across; the other jerked up, indicating ... Not Rudi, as I had expected. Hans, who was leaning over Leif's shoulder trying to see the board.

If I had planned a spot of nocturnal spying, I'd rather have had Hans on my trail than Rudi. The latter was much more intelligent. However, Hans was much bigger. It was a moot point, and I figured John had his reasons.

Rudi announced "distract," with a thick Viennese accent. He was getting into the swing of it, rolling his *r*'s with fine effect. Max's brow furrowed. It was beginning to dawn on him that he might be missing some nuance or other.

I spelled "initiame," slapping down the tiles with reckless haste, before Max could call the game off. It was the best I could do. I couldn't find two *t*'s. John stared at me in consternation, while I thought the word at him as hard as I could. I don't know whether the ESP worked, or whether his quick mind made the right connection. He said, "Nothing," with crisp emphasis, and looked at his tiles. "Nothing," he repeated sadly. "What a rotten collection of useless consonants."

"Initiame," Rudi said. "Wait—that is not a word. She is cheating."

He sounded shocked.

"Enough," Max said. "I am weary of your tricks, Smythe. Come here and sit for me. I am desirous of adding your portrait to my collection."

Peter Lorre couldn't have done it better—the long hiss of the sibilants, the faint, derisive smile. But the paper he finally selected was black. John didn't appear to be visibly heartened by this; he gave me a very thoughtful look before moving to obey Max.

I collected the scattered tiles and folded the board. We had not had much time, but it had helped. Max was a subordinate, who had no authority to initiate action. Before calling off the dig, he would have to contact his boss. That meant we had a little more time.

As I finished packing up the game, the door burst open and Georg Hasseltine came in, carrying a wooden crate. He was alone; no guard for Georg. His gaze wandered over the room, ignoring his brother's raised hand with unconscious cruelty, and focused on me.

"There you are, Dr. Bliss. I have been looking for you." He put the box on the table and pushed his glasses back onto the bridge of his nose. "You will appreciate what I have found."

It took all my willpower to be civil to the little creep, but one never knows when civility will pay off. Besides, I was curious. Max wasn't; he went on cutting. He knew that whatever Georg had found, it was not the treasure.

To an inexperienced eye—mine, in this case—the objects Georg placed tenderly on the table might have come from a garbage pile: two lumps of corroded metal, a roughly shaped stone, and a handful of bones, brown and brittle with age. The young man stood gazing down on this unsightly assemblage with shining eyes. He looked little older than his true age as enthusiasm warmed his features. My irresponsible emotions veered from contempt to pity.

"You see?" Georg said eagerly. "You realize what it means?"

Leif got up and joined us, closely followed by the faithful Hans. "What is it, Georg?" he asked.

"You wouldn't understand." Georg continued to beam at me. "Isn't it wonderful?"

My sympathies veered back, due north. "I don't understand either," I said coolly. "I'm not an archaeologist, and the Iron Age isn't my bag."

Georg pounded on the give-away word. "I knew you would recognize them."

"Only that this is iron." I picked up one of the metal lumps. As I turned it in the light, it took on form. "Arrowhead?" I hazarded.

"More probably a point from a throwing spear. That isn't definitive; a wandering hunter could have lost it. But the bones are those of domesticated animals—sheep and cattle. The spindle whorl proves my case."

There was no point in pretending to be dense. If I didn't say it, he would. "Kitchen midden," I said.

"Yes. And that means habitation—probably a farm or fort. A rich settlement."

"Rich?" Max rose, knuckles on the desk. "How do you know that?"

"It's a prime location," Georg answered. "Easy to defend, with its own water supply and ample pasturage. A coveted site. Only a strong leader could hold it. Probably a local chieftain or jarl."

"But the treasure," Max said. "Where would they have hidden it?"

Georg lifted one shoulder and smiled at me—one intellectual to another, deploring the ignorance of the hoi polloi. "The treasure is unimportant. I suspect that this—"

"Unimportant?" Max's voice was very quiet, but it wiped the smile from Georg's lips. "What do you think we are here for, you young fool? If you have learned anything from your digging, you had better tell me at once, or—"

"Wait." Leif moved quickly, putting himself between the angry little man and Georg. "Let me talk to him. He will tell me."

"Talk, then. Persuade him. If you fail, there are other methods."

Georg appeared shaken. Maybe his last fix was wearing off. He allowed Leif to lead him out.

John edged toward the door. "Excuse me," he murmured. "I know it's frightfully early, but . . ."

"Go, then. All of you—except you, Dr. Bliss. I wish to talk with you."

John didn't favor me with a glance or a good-night. He ambled out, followed by Rudi. When the door had closed behind them, Max let out a long sigh.

"Please sit down, Dr. Bliss. You have nothing to fear from me. I think we can help one another."

I took the chair he indicated. Max turned to the window and stood staring out, hands clasped behind his back. I glanced at the desk. He had almost finished the silhouette. It was a gentler caricature than I would have expected; he had turned John's admittedly pointed nose into a modified Pinocchio pecker and made his chin recede more than it actually did, but that was all. Hand and scissors had slipped, perhaps when Georg said the magic word "rich." A ragged tear ran across the shadow head, from the bridge of the nose to where the ear would have been.

Max turned from the window, once more calm and smiling. "Let us not waste time sparring with one another, Dr. Bliss. You are an intelligent woman, and I am a very busy man. It would serve the interests of both of us if I could conclude this matter swiftly and leave you in peace."

I didn't say anything, but he interpreted my expression accurately. "You doubt that I would leave you alive and well? Consider the pros and cons. I have nothing to gain by harming you and your friends, and a great deal to lose.

I will even make concessions, if it will ease your mind. For instance, I might restore Mr. Jonsson to you."

"So far as I can see, that concession would just make it simpler for you," I said. "Get all the pigeons in the same place, so to speak."

"But if you had a gun," Max said softly. "A thirty-eight, fully loaded? Picture it. You and Mr. Jonsson, locked in one of the upstairs rooms. We could not reach you from the window, but you could see us leave—and you could shoot to kill if anyone tried to enter by the door."

Talk about your seductive pictures. What's more, some odd sixth sense told me he was sincere—not planning any nasty little tricks like setting fire to the house. Watching the play of emotions on my face, Max sidled up to the desk and lowered himself into a chair. "I will consider any reasonable suggestion," he murmured. "Only help me to find the treasure."

"I don't know where it is," I wailed.

"But you are the possessor of expert knowledge, training, that might give me a clue." His voice changed. It held a note of purely human curiosity. "How the devil did Smythe trick you into joining him in this? Your reputation is excellent, and now that I have met you I find it impossible to believe you wanted to swindle Mr. Jonsson."

"It's too complicated to explain," I said mournfully. "But you're right—he did trick me, the bastard."

"He will be punished. For that and other injudicious acts."

"I don't suppose you'd include him in your amnesty offer."

"No. Why should you care? You owe him nothing; he is responsible for your present plight."

"How true."

"Are you in love with him?"

"No. None of your business."

"I take a fatherly interest."

I gaped at him. He went on seriously, "He is not a proper associate for a lady of your worth. You will be better off without him. Mr. Hasseltine, now—there is a fine man, young and healthy. What are your feelings for him?"

My head was spinning. I couldn't believe I was getting advice on affairs of the heart from a leader of organized crime. Uncle Maxie's Love Column . . .

"Now, look here, Max," I said. "Not that I don't appreciate your interest—but let's get back to basics, okay? Your deal has its attractive points, and I'd be strongly tempted to take you up on it, except for one detail."

"Your professional conscience?"

"Well . . . I hate what you're planning to do. My training and my moral senses are howling with outrage. But there isn't one artifact in existence that I'd place above a human life. Especially mine."

"Then what is the difficulty?"

He still sounded like kindly old Uncle Maxie, weary but patient. I waved my arms wildly. "Max, I don't have the information! Georg is the archaeologist; I've just enough background to think he may be right in his assessment of the site. There may have been a fifth-century house here, with all the attendant features—outbuildings, a defensive wall, maybe a cemetery. If the graves weren't robbed in antiquity, they might contain all kinds of goodies—like the chalice. It's equally possible that the chalice was one object in a cache of treasures buried by the owner in time of war for safekeeping. If you had a couple of trained scholars on the spot, with the necessary equipment, they could plot the site and locate the cemetery. But there's no way on earth anybody could pinpoint the location of a cache. Where would you bury your savings, if you were in the ancient owner's position? In the farmyard? Under the living-room floor? In the pigsty? Damn it, Max, even if we had a complete plan of the house and outbuildings, we still wouldn't have a clue. It's hopeless. Why don't you give up and go home?"

Elbow on the table, chin propped on his hand, Max listened attentively to my peroration.

"I am tempted to tell you why," he said when I finished talking, breathless and flushed. "Better still, I am tempted to show you. Wait here."

Naturally I waited. I couldn't take my eyes off the mutilated silhouette. The tear was like a ragged wound.

Max was back in a few minutes, carrying a manila envelope. He opened it and handed me the contents.

They were color photographs, eight-by-ten in size. Six of them—sides, top, and bottom. The object was shaped like a little house, with the roof sloping up to a richly ornamented ridgepole—a doll's house, about a foot long. But doll's houses, even royal doll's houses, aren't made of gold. Insets of scarlet and blue enamel, in a convoluted interlace pattern, studded the sides and roof. It had been beautifully restored—at least I assumed it had, for a thing like that couldn't have been buried for fifteen centuries without getting battered.

"So this is it," I murmured. "Funny. I postulated its existence, but never once visualized what it might be like. It's . . . nice, isn't it?"

"Does it alter your image of the honest Scandinavian farmer?" Max asked with a cynical smile.

"It's a reliquary," I said. "Probably Celtic. I admit you wouldn't expect to find a Christian church or monastery in this area so early—but that doesn't prove this was raiders' loot. Maybe he got it in trade, or bought it, or—or something."

"You cling stubbornly to your preconceptions," Max said, amused.

I wasn't sure myself why I resented the suggestion that the fifth-century lord of the island was a barbaric burner of churches. He wasn't my ancestor; probably he wasn't Gus's ancestor either, despite the latter's claim. And so what if he was? Nobody's ancestors are perfect.

"It doesn't matter," I said, shrugging my fantasies aside.

"No. What does matter is the quality of the hoard. If the two objects found thus far are representative—and we can assume they are, since they were discovered by accident—then it is worth a great deal of trouble to me."

"Granted. But the treasure is looking more and more like a cache; you wouldn't expect to find something like this reliquary in a pagan grave. Which makes your chances of finding it remote. Would I be rudely intruding into classified matters if I asked where you got this?"

"What you really mean is why didn't we ask the thief to draw us a map." Max spoke lightly, but I had hit a sore point. His hands began to move restlessly around the desk, as if they ached to be holding scissors and paper. "I see no reason why I shouldn't tell you. We have not been able to locate the original finder. It could have been anyone—a farmhand, a trespasser, a hunter, a pair of lovers seeking privacy. The man we dealt with was several steps removed from the finder, and unfortunately the member of our organization who purchased the reliquary from him was too dense to see the implications. Not until it was viewed by one of our consultants did these emerge."

"You can't blame the poor man," I said soothingly. "It's pretty damned farfetched, Max. Only a specialist in Scandinavian antiquities would make the connection."

"Yes, we were told that much when we questioned the seller a second time." Max saw my lips tighten, and went on quickly, "The only useful thing that emerged was his admission that he had not come to us first. When I heard Smythe's name, I knew he was the man to follow. He has a number of annoying qualities, but he is without peer in his own field."

With some self-disgust I realized I had been enjoying the conversation. The insights I had gained were interesting and possibly useful, but that wasn't the reason why I found myself chatting away in such a relaxed fashion. The strange little man had a certain something. You couldn't call it charm; you certainly couldn't call it integrity. But there was unquestionably rapport between us, a sense that under far different circumstances we might have been friends. Even now, I think Max really did like me.

"I'd help if I could," I said, and halfway meant it.

"Then talk to Smythe." Max leaned forward, his eyes intent. "In my business one develops an instinct for such matters. I think he knows more than he admits. Find out what it is. If you succeed, you shall have your Mr. Jonsson and all the security you wish."

The interview was at an end. I found my own way out. Max was reaching for his scissors when I left the room. I don't know what he used for a subject.

Chapter Eight

I WENT STRAIGHT to the front door and out of the house, without making any attempt to conceal my movements. I wanted Max to think that the discussion had inspired me to have another look at the site. I definitely intended to do that, but it wasn't my only purpose.

The air was crisp and winy. The sun hung low in the west, and the sky was emblazoned like a page from a medieval manuscript, gold and copper, crimson and bronze. The light was more than adequate. In fact, it couldn't have been better. Slanting shadows can show up topographical features that are obscured by growth.

I went around the house into the barnyard. The big barn was a beauty, probably older than the house, and built of local stone. It would have served nicely as a fortress in time of war. Well tended as it was, it looked desolate without the cattle and horses that had once occupied the stalls. As I approached, I saw Pierre sitting on the ground, his back against the wall and his rifle on his knees. He nodded and said politely, *"Bonsoir, mademoiselle."*

I nodded back and went on, following the eastern shoreline. It was a lovely walk, through the meadows at sunset, with waves sloshing softly among the reeds. When the ground started to get soggy, I headed inland. Reaching the pasture, I climbed onto a rock and had a look around. The only breaks in the yellowing stubble were the pits dug by the treasure hunters. Georg's neat little brown square made a rather pathetic intrusion.

Maybe it was just my imagination, but as I surveyed the pasture I began to see things. The mowing had been done roughly, inexpertly, but the bare bones of the land showed through, and the shadows were long and sharp. To the north, in front of the trees—surely that line of shadow was more regular than one cast by a natural feature. It defined a low bank, broken in places, but distinct. And toward the northeast a patch of brighter green, roughly oval, where the grass had grown thicker and richer than elsewhere. . . .

A little thrill ran through me. If I could see it, how much more would it have affected Georg, who was the real expert? Was it pure luck that had prompted him to select the site of the ancient garbage dump, or had he seen something that gave him a clue?

John must have seen it too. I felt certain that this was not his first visit to the island. It wouldn't have been easy to trespass unobserved when Gus was in residence, but it could have been managed; Gus kept no cattle, so the pasture would be deserted most of the time. I did not underestimate John's expertise. I had no idea what his background was; he might even have a degree in archaeology.

And the plan was typical of his cautious, wily mind. A perfectly open, orthodox dig, sponsored by Gus and supervised by John, who could undoubtedly have produced a briefcase full of academic credentials if they were required. As the man in charge he could control every detail of the digging. It took a trained eye to recognize the value of a battered, corroded object wrenched from the dirt; silver rots, gold is bent and twisted. Yes, he would be in a perfect position to extract the plums from the pudding, and to make off with the loot and have it replaced by copies. "My laboratory at the university can restore this. . . ."

Only, instead of a greedy, gullible property owner, he had found Gus. No doubt he had been in disguise when he made the first approach—glasses, an academic stoop, a hesitant little cough. Gus had turned him down flat, and then the tricky skunk had thought of me.

The outlines were clear now, and for some illogical reason they made me feel a little more kindly toward John. He had no scruples about using me in his swindle, but he had not intended to drag me into the middle of a shooting war. Georg and Leif were, as he had insisted, inconvenient leftovers from a former scam, and John himself hadn't known about Max's group until he saw the silhouette. I had to give the bastard credit; he had tried to persuade me to leave.

I climbed down from the rock and began pacing back and forth across the pasture, trying to emulate an archaeologist—or an ignoramus's idea of an archaeologist. I assumed someone was following me. I would have had someone follow me, if I had been Max. So I picked up a stick and jabbed it into the ground from time to time, and then bent over to examine the turf. I must say the procedure increased my respect for the diggers. Thickly matted roots made a crust as hard as a plank.

My path led eventually toward the belt of trees on the north. They were pines, high enough and thick enough to frustrate the growth of weeds and brambles. The ground was covered with needles that gave off a faint sweet smell as my feet pressed them. A spectral greenish light permeated the grove, and even the birds were still. I didn't go far into the trees. I had the feeling that something was watching me, and that it wasn't one of Max's men. Though I still carried the stick, I did not probe the ground. If anybody was under there, I didn't want to disturb him.

I had planned to pick up my pace at this point, but I must admit I moved faster than I had originally intended. The soft sighing sounds I heard were undoubtedly produced by the wind stirring the boughs. In that soft false twilight they conveyed quite another impression.

At a brisk trot, I followed the treeline westward. Before long the roof of the shack came into sight. I headed straight for it, running.

He popped out from behind a tree, waving his rifle in an unprofessional manner. Max wasn't the only one who was showing signs of strain in the rustic ambience.

"Halt," he said breathlessly. It wasn't Hans, it was the Austrian, a husky specimen with scant sandy hair.

"I've halted. Had I but known you were here, I would not have ventured to intrude." It didn't come out quite so smoothly; I was out of breath too. Seeing him frown, I went on in German. "I was looking at the site. Max asked me to help him."

"Go back now."

"If you say so."

"Drop the stick."

"Stick? It's only a little—"

"Drop it. *Schnell, schnell.*"

I didn't know whether to be flattered or insulted. I don't mind being considered brave, but I was not stupid enough to go in swinging a stick against an opponent armed with a rifle. So I dropped the stick, *schnell,* and backed away.

I had seen all I needed to see. There was no building of any sort on the east side of the island. Though I had not explored the northern side thoroughly—and I was not about to, except in broad daylight—the hut was the only place I had found that might serve as a prison. It was small, perhaps a shelter for a herdsman or shepherd in the days when Gus's ancestors had practiced animal husbandry, and, like everything else Gus owned, it had been kept in good repair. A shiny new padlock hung from the hasp on the door. There was only one window, and it was covered by a wooden shutter.

When I got to the barnyard Pierre was still there. Max was with him; as I strolled up, he turned on me in visible exasperation. "Where have you been? It is late."

"I wanted to have a look at the site."

"Anything?"

"Only what I expected."

"No more exploring," Max said, like a stern parent. "You should be in your bed."

"Okay," I said amiably.

Max followed me as I walked toward the house, shaking his finger and lecturing. "I expect you to stay inside tonight. In your own wing of the house."

"Okay."

"My men will be on guard, outside and in. No one is to leave."

"Okay, okay."

"Go straight to your room."

"Can I get a snack first?"

"Oh, very well. But be quick about it."

"I'll take it to my room."

He trailed along. Maybe he was hoping I'd suggest a congenial chat over a cup of coffee. I didn't. I piled a tray with bottles of beer, cheese, bread, and sausages. Max watched, eyes widening as the comestibles piled up, but he made no comment until I poured milk into a bowl and stooped to put it on the floor.

"For the cat?" he asked.

"No, it's for the pixies."

"Perhaps it does not like milk," Max said seriously. "Marguerite will not touch it."

"Marguerite sounds like one damned spoiled cat."

Max was offended. "Are you finished?" he asked stiffly.

"I guess so." I hefted the tray with the never-to-be-forgotten skill I had acquired one summer as a waitress at Joe's Café, and went out.

The wing in which our rooms were located was connected to the central block by a door from which a corridor led straight down the length of the wing, with doors on either side. Rudi had taken up a position by the connecting door. He stiffened to attention when his boss appeared, his gun at the ready. The velvet armchair in which he was sitting detracted slightly from the picture of military discipline, but one could hardly blame him for wanting to be comfortable if he was going to be there all night.

He looked yearningly at my loaded tray, and Max, who missed very little, said sharply, "You will take no food or drink from her."

"But of course not," Rudi said, as if the idea had never occurred to him.

I swayed on down the corridor. (Carrying a tray necessitates a certain rhythm of the hips. At least that was the custom at Joe's.) John emerged from the bathroom, timing his exit with such precision that we met just outside the door.

"Any time now," he said, out of the corner of his mouth. Max trotted up, ears pricked; John turned the twist of his mouth into a leer and gave me a long vertical inspection, from head to foot.

"A little late-night supper à *deux?*" he inquired. "What a super idea. Who's the lucky lad?"

"Not you," said Max indignantly. "Get into your room and do not leave it."

"But what if I have to get up during the night to—"

Max shoved him into his room and slammed the door. "What a tedious person he is," he remarked. I could not but agree.

Since John was a master at double entendres of all varieties, I took his comments to indicate approval of the plan I had cleverly concocted. I could not be sure whether he had indicated Leif or Hans when he spelled out "distract," but by keeping the former in situ (to use an archaeological term), I could immobilize Hans at the same time. I assumed the latter was outside. The doors and windows were the only exits from the bedrooms, and Rudi was covering the doors.

"Mr. Hasseltine is in this room," Max said helpfully, indicating the door.

"You are becoming a trifle tedious yourself, Max," I said. "Get lost, will you? Rudi is audience enough."

Max removed himself. I kicked the door. After a minute Leif opened it. "You," he exclaimed.

"Me," I agreed. "I thought you might be feeling a bit peckish."

"Peckish?"

"Speak German. I understand it, you know."

Smiling, he took the tray, ushered me inside, and

kicked the door shut, in one movement. "What a pleasant idea. We may as well take what enjoyment we can from the situation."

"I hope you don't think I am being forward," I said. "To be truthful, I felt the need of companionship. I'm very nervous."

"Of course you are." He put the tray on a table and gallantly helped me into a chair. "But I'm sure we have nothing to worry about, Vicky. Max has taken a fancy to you—which is not surprising."

This went on for a while—me expressing girlish timidity, Leif manfully reassuring me—while we drank beer and ate cheese. Gradually the light faded to a soft gray twilight, but the darkness I had hoped for did not come. The only encouraging note was the fact that Hans was indeed distracted. The curtains at the window fluttered in the breeze; every now and then a bundle of fingers shaped like sausages would catch at a blowing fold to keep it out of the line of vision.

When Leif set his empty bottle down with a decisive thump and wiped the crumbs off his lips, I knew the second stage of the entertainment—the part Hans was waiting for—was about to begin. Leif rose from his chair. With slow, deliberate strides he came to me and held out his hands. I gave him mine. He lifted me into his arms.

It may have been the change in language. People sound much more formal when they speak a tongue that is not their own unless they speak it fluently. They even act more formally, as if constrained by the necessity of thinking what word to use next. The hands that fondled me, the lips that explored mine might have belonged to a stranger, not the big ox who had mauled me in the park in Stockholm. I was decidedly short of breath and very, very cooperative when he picked me up, as easily as he might have lifted a child, and carried me toward the bed.

I am a declared feminist, but I have never believed that economic and political equality (which we're a helluva long way from having, by the way) should have anything to do with the relations between the sexes—the romantic aspects, as Schmidt would have said. Like every other woman I cherish secret fantasies. My favorite is to be short. I dreamed of having a man hold me close, with my cheek resting on his chest, not his ear. Of feeling the steady, passionate beat of his heart, not his bristly beard. Of having his lips pressed against my hair, not the other way around.

Now I was living my fantasy, and I didn't like it.

Also, I couldn't concentrate on the matter at hand. I kept thinking of Gus, languishing in his dank, dirty prison; of John, prowling the grounds; of Hans, who was probably halfway in the room by now, the lousy Peeping Tom. . . .

"I can't," I gasped, and rolled off the far side of the bed.

"Liebchen, mein Schatz, mein Herzliebchen—"

"Yes, right," I gabbled, tucking my blouse into my jeans. "I'm sorry, Leif, I'm really sorry. I can't stand it, it's too much. Max is probably going to shoot me tomorrow or the next day, and Hans is watching every move we make, and I—I'm just not in the mood, dammit."

In case he harbored any doubts as to my sincerity, I burst into tears.

The flood quenched Leif's ardor. Possibly the idea of providing a free peepshow for Hans didn't appeal to him either. He was very nice. He patted me and told me to get a good night's sleep. "I promise you, on my honor, that you will not be harmed," he said solemnly. "And when this is over—"

"Yes. Oh, yes, Leif . . . No, Leif. Remember Hans."

Somehow I made it back to my room, trying not to see Rudi's knowing grin. My hands were shaking so badly it seemed to take forever to get out of my clothes and into my nightgown. I was disgusted with myself, but I couldn't help it. The night air felt bitterly cold. Even after I had gotten into bed and pulled the covers up to my chin I couldn't stop shivering.

I was reluctant to close the shutters, even though it was still exasperatingly light outside and Hans was on the prowl. I could hear the crunch of gravel under his feet as he walked up and down. I assumed—I hoped—John had managed to get out while Hans was playing voyeur. I wondered how he planned to get back in. Maybe he had counted on me to keep up the distraction. Too bad. There are limits.

I was still awake, twisting and turning, when I heard an outrageous burst of noise outside—a shrill caterwauling of animal rage, a deeper howl that sounded equally inhuman. Heavy footsteps pounded along the path. My curtains billowed and a dark form slid into the room and fell across my feet.

"Scream," John said breathlessly. "It won't take him long to—"

"You're squashing my legs."

"Scream, damn it!" He grabbed a handful of my nightie and tried to tear it. I defy Muhammad Ali to rend a wad of Dacron; it just stretches, interminably. John swore, I started to laugh—an insane, high-pitched giggle that afflicts me in times of stress. He flung back the covers and swung the rest of his body into the bed. I yelped. His feet were bare, and as cold and clammy as those of a corpse.

"Louder and faster," said my seducer. I obliged with a series of shrieks, ranging from "Rape" to "Fire." The response was gratifyingly prompt. It was nice to know I need not fear being raped or set on fire in that house. Killed, maybe, but not sexually molested or immolated.

Rudi was the first to arrive. He had the presence of mind to switch on the light. Max and Leif were right behind him; they all stared. John had his hand over my mouth, to keep me from laughing, and I was wriggling as I tried to get his elbow out of my stomach.

I squirmed out from under him and sat up. His dark slacks and sweater were dry, but his skin had the slimy dankness of a fish's scales. When I saw Leif's face I stopped laughing. He came at the bed in a rush. I bounded up and threw myself in front of John, who had prudently retired into the farthest-possible corner. He made no attempt to prevent me.

The bed, and Max's shout, brought Leif to a stop. Veins bulged in his forehead. "I will kill him," he said quietly.

"Not you," Max corrected. "Where is that stupid . . . Hans!"

Hans was stuck in the window. Lacking the sense to turn sideways, he just stood there grunting and shoving. Max pointed out his options, in words that clanked like ice cubes, and Hans climbed into the room. His cheek was bleeding freely from a long row of parallel scratches. His face went blank with disbelief when he saw John.

"How did he get here?"

"I was about to ask you the same question," Max said through his teeth.

Now that the tension had subsided somewhat, John considered that it was safe to come out from behind my skirts.

"He turned his back for a few moments," he said, with a patronizing smile. "That was all I needed."

"You turned your back?" Max said to Hans.

Hans turned pink, like an embarrassed baby. He had very fair skin. *"Aber, Herr Max—die Dame war hier im Zimmer, und da war das Fenster, and wenn sie aus dem Fenster geschaut hätte . . ."*

"That shows a delicate mind, Hans," I said. "I appreciate it."

"Und," Hans went on, indignation replacing modesty, *"die Katze hat mich—"*

"Herr Gott allmächtig!" Max shouted. Then he got a grip on himself and inquired carefully, "How long ago did this—turning of your back occur?"

"Not long, Herr Max, not long at all. Only a few moments ago."

"Hmph." Max's frown lessened a trifle. "Then no great harm has been done. However, I grow weary of Mr. Smythe's frivolities. I think the time has come. . . ." He paused, his eyes moving deliberately over each of us in turn. My mouth went dry. "Max," I said.

"Hans," Max said.

John tried to get behind me again. Hans's heavy hand fell on his shoulder and yanked him out into the open.

"Take him to the cellar," Max said.

John's face turned a pale shade of green. His complexion was the only part of him he couldn't control; when he spoke, his voice was steady. "Don't do anything you might regret, Max."

"I thought as much." Max folded his arms. "You have information."

"A tidbit or two. I've been saving them for an emergency. It appears," John said wryly, "that the emergency is upon me. I'm ready for a trade."

"You are in no position to bargain. The cellar, Hans."

"You'll get no cooperation from me if you go through with this, Max," I said. My voice was not at all steady.

"I regret." Max gestured. Hans transferred his grip to John's arm and shoved him toward the door. The audience had grown to include Georg, who had observed the proceedings with a singularly unattractive smile.

"I'll come along," he said, baring a few more teeth. "I would enjoy watching."

"Georg!" his brother exclaimed.

"Watching is about all you're capable of doing," John said rudely. "You ineffectual, effeminate, impotent little junkie."

He could have avoided the blow. Georg telegraphed his punch, and his coordination was shot to hell. In fact, it appeared to me that at the last moment John leaned into it. Georg's fist landed on his cheekbone and John went limp, as gracefully as Errol Flynn in the grasp of the Inquisition.

I sat down. There didn't seem to be anything else I could do.

ii

I should have worn the rest of the night away pacing and wringing my hands. Actually, my eyes closed the minute I lay down, and I slept like a baby. The weather may have been partially responsible. When I woke, the room was in shadow; clouds hung heavy in the sky and a sharp wind snapped the curtains.

I rolled over and reached for the hard object that was poking into my hip. It was a round, squat bottle, made of dark plastic and carrying a pharmacist's label. "Multivitamins," the label said. I shook it experimentally. There was no rattle of capsules, only the shifting of some nonliquid substance.

Thoughtfully I tucked the bottle into my bra and pulled on a heavy sweater to hide the bulge. By the time I was ready to appear in public, my imagination had gotten into gear, and I was feeling . . . Well, let's say I felt a little queasy. It wasn't hard to figure out what John was up to; he would remain resolutely unconscious as long as possible and dribble out his information as slowly as was compatible with safety. He was trying to gain time. I hoped his plan had worked.

I found him in the kitchen scrambling eggs, and I am not ashamed to admit that I was relieved to see him. On the counter beside him was the cat, eating bacon with the insolence of a creature who knows he is under official protection. I might have known John's attempt to woo the cat with kidneys had an ulterior motive. He had used it, quite cold-bloodedly, to complete the distraction of Hans, but it really hadn't been in danger; a big, stupid man is no match for an angry feline, especially when the big, stupid man knows his boss has a weakness for pussycats. Hans was still nursing a grudge. He fingered the scratches on his cheek as he glowered at the cat.

They were all there, even Georg and Leif—sitting at the table waiting for breakfast. The condemned man was not eating a hearty meal, he was cooking it for the executioners.

I said, "Good morning," and John turned. I examined him critically.

"You got off easier than I expected," I said.

"Most of the bruises are in places that don't show," John explained. "How about slicing some bacon?"

I took the knife. His wrist was swollen to twice normal

size, and turning a pretty shade of purple.

"Let me do that," Leif said, as I leaned into the slab of bacon. I handed over the knife. "Did you sleep well?" he asked tenderly.

"Yes, as a matter of fact." John glared at me. I went on, "I take it you have arrived at an agreement."

"Oh, right," John said. "I've agreed to show them where the loot is buried and they have agreed to cut my throat. Amiable arrangement, isn't it?"

"I will keep my promise, Dr. Bliss," Max said. "In a few hours you will be free of us."

The stench of burning eggs filled the kitchen. John dumped them onto a platter with such vigor that fragments flew all around. "Don't get your hopes up, Max, my lad," he said. "As I told you, I'm no surveyor. The calculations are going to take a little time."

"As much time as you can manage," Max said with a sneer. "Don't get *your* hopes up, my friend. Dr. Hasseltine will be happy to assist you in your calculations."

Georg, devouring burned eggs with the relish of a man whose taste buds are dead and buried, looked up. Apparently he had not been present during the interrogation after all, for he asked, "You know the bearings?"

"Rough ones," John replied. "My informant didn't have equipment with him; he had to estimate."

"Naturally," Georg said. "To obtain accurate measurements on such uneven terrain, one would need levels, transit and tripod, plumb bob. . . . I can perhaps rig some sort of makeshift substitute."

"That would be most accommodating of you," Max said. "And the sooner we begin, the sooner we will be finished."

"Why don't you just kill him now and get it over with?" I said angrily. "This cat-and-mouse nonsense—"

"Keep your suggestions to yourself," John said.

"We must make sure he has not tricked us," Max explained. "I promised him a pleasant death if he would cooperate. I will keep my word, but if he has deceived me . . ."

"That does it," John announced. Picking up the heavy frying pan, he tossed it into the sink with a theatrical gesture. "I've had it. No more Mr. Nice Guy. No more cooking, no more delectable dishes—"

"Thank heaven for that," Max said, poking at the shreds of burned egg. "Come. To work."

Chapter Nine

THERE WAS a purposefulness to Max's procedures that morning that had been lacking before. Until I saw what he could do in the way of organization I did not fully realize how uncharacteristically indecisive his earlier actions had been. For the past twenty-four hours he had just been marking time. If he hadn't known it before, one look at the pasture would have told him that random digging was no use. I could think of several reasons why he had been willing to waste time, and I didn't like any of them. I disliked his brisk, angry efficiency even more. Today was the day. If John's revelations turned out to be a red herring, Max would pack it up and leave—after he had finished his other business. We had at the most about twelve hours.

John had reached the same conclusion. His seemingly erratic behavior had one purpose—delay. He was hoping for darkness—twilight, rather—before making his attempt to escape. I was pessimistic about his chances. Twelve hours is a long time.

Nagged by Max, Georg collected the equipment he proposed to use. It wasn't impressive; the stakes and string and other implements resembled gardening tools, and were, in fact, taken from the shed that served that function. At Max's pressing invitation I joined the group and we left the house.

The sky threatened, and a chill breeze denied the approach of midsummer. I demanded a coat, and Max let me go up to get it. When I returned he glanced at the purse I had slung over my shoulder, but did not object; he had searched it himself and knew I had no weapon.

When we reached the pasture, everyone stared expectantly at Max. The wind that ruffled John's flaxen locks and blew my hair into my eyes didn't stir a strand of Max's gray wig. He took a paper out of his breast pocket, studied it, and turned a minatory eye on John.

"Fifteen paces due west from the large boulder at the northeast corner. Fifty paces due south. Sixteen paces west from the dead pine on the southeast corner, fifty paces due north from there. Is that it?"

"I told you it was rough," John said defensively.

It was also straight out of "The Gold Bug" or some other fiction. Perhaps Max had not been raised on the classics. He was skeptical, though; as his chilly gaze remained fixed on John, the latter shivered exaggeratedly and wrapped both arms around his body. "The second set of measurements is obviously a cross-bearing," he added.

Georg shook his head and made disapproving noises. "It is very inaccurate. How long is a pace? There are too many boulders; which is the correct one? And I cannot believe that none of you had the intelligence to bring a compass."

Mine was in my purse at that very moment, disguised as the butt end of a flashlight. At least one of Gus's boats must have direction-finding apparatus, but since none of the gang had thought of that, I didn't see any reason to bring it up.

The men scattered, looking for landmarks. There was no dead pine at the southeast corner. Finally someone found a stump and concluded that must be the remains of the tree. Georg sat down on the stump, took out notebook and pencil, and began making calculations, muttering, "If we take it that true north lies that way . . ."

The proceedings had a certain macabre humor, but I was in no mood to enjoy them. "I'm going for a walk," I told Max. "It's freezing."

"Stay away from the hut," Max said curtly. His eyes were on John, who, closely followed by Rudi, was pretending to look for a boulder. They wouldn't let him out of their sight from now on.

The hut didn't interest me. Gus wasn't there. The Austrian had been following me the day before. Max had ordered him to give the impression that he was guarding the hut if I seemed to be interested in it, but he had had to run to get there before I did.

I was almost certain I knew where they were keeping Gus, but almost wasn't good enough. If I was wrong, there might not be time for a second guess. So I went into the forest.

It had been eerie before, in the dimness of twilight. Under a stormy sky, with wind lashing the upper branches, it was a perfect setting for a horror film. One expected to see the Frankenstein monster come lurching along between the trees.

The search didn't take long, since I was looking for a man-made structure. I found a few blocks of dressed stone, tumbled by the growth of tree roots that had heaved them to the surface. Man had left his mark, but not in the recent past. The blocks might have lined a grave.

When I emerged from the trees onto the headland above the water, the wind blew my hair back like a banner. It was a north wind, carrying the snowy breath of the high mountains. Thirty feet below, waves attacked the tumbled rocks of a shallow bay. The cliff wasn't sheer; in fact, it could hardly be called a cliff—just a steep decline, half rock, half earth, with clumps of rough weeds clinging to pockets of soil. I wondered if Gus could get down, with his game leg. It was the only place I had seen that offered possible hiding places, among the wave-washed rocks. As for swimming—the steel-gray water, laced with dirty white froth, was not enticing.

I started back. I must have been midway through the belt of trees before I suddenly realized that I wasn't nervous any longer. The shadowed aisles between the trunks promised shelter from wind and storm, not hiding places for monsters. The moan of the boughs overhead stirred my blood instead of chilling it. The trees might guard the crumbling bones of the ancient dead, but the spirits of those antique warriors and herdsmen held no terrors for me. They had accepted me as one of their own.

I arrived at the dig in the middle of a loud, abusive argument. The digging had not yet begun, and the first words I heard, from Max, explained the delay.

"What use are your mathematics?" he shouted at Georg. "You are wrong. Your cross-bearings come nowhere near one another."

"I made a slight error," Georg muttered. "If you will try these new calculations—"

Max slapped his notebook from his hand. "The man who found the reliquary did not use exact measurements. We will imitate his method. We will pace off—"

"But you don't know the length of his stride," Georg protested, with some justification.

"No matter. You—no, you, Willy." The Austrian started nervously when Max pointed at him. "Go to the boulder. Then walk normally. Count as you go and stop when you reach fifteen."

It had taken them almost an hour to arrive at this common-sense solution. There is an adage dear to strategists: Divide and conquer. Confuse and conquer is an even better technique.

"I think there's a cemetery in the woods," I said brightly.

"Later, later." Max waved me to silence.

"I think I'll go back to the house."

"Later. Are you at the boulder, Willy? Good. Start walking. One—two—three—"

"I could make some coffee," I said. "Mr. Smythe looks as if he could use a stimulant."

I shouldn't have mentioned his name. Max had become sensitized; the syllables stung him like a hornet.

"No!" he cried, turning to me. "Don't speak to him; don't go near him. Be quiet. You are distracting me. Curse it, Willy; how far have you gotten?"

Willy was standing stiffly at attention, arms at his sides. "Fifteen, sir."

"Good. Good. You are sure you counted correctly? Then turn—a right-angle turn. Fifty paces."

Willy started off in measured slow step, like the Marines at a funeral procession. The formal deliberation of his movements had a hypnotic effect; I found myself counting in chorus with Max: "Forty-nine, fifty." Max shrieked, "Stop!" with such shrill vehemence that Willy leaped into the air.

"Stand still," Max shouted. "Don't move. If you stir one inch, under any circumstances whatever, I will skin you alive. Now." He turned a measuring eye on the remainder of his crew. According to their temperaments they shrank or stiffened under his survey. Hans giggled nervously.

"Not you," Max said, scowling at him. "Rudi, you are the same height. The tree stump. Go to it."

Rudi plodded off through the stubble. "You are welcome to stay here, Dr. Bliss," Max said, without looking at me. "But you must not try to speak privately with Smythe. Is that clear?"

"It's clear, yes. But I don't see why—"

"Dr. Bliss, you cannot suppose—"

"I am here, Max," Rudi called.

"I see you are, cretin. Stay there." Max took my arm and led me away from the others. "Dr. Bliss," he said earnestly, "don't suppose that I am unaware of your intentions. You will not give up attempting to save the life of that wretched man until the deed is done. I understand your principles, and I admire them. I don't want to see you hurt. Do you believe that?"

"Oddly enough, I do believe it," I admitted.

"However, I am a man of business. I must obey . . . That is, I must obey the dictates of professional necessity. If you interfere with my plans, I will remove you from my path. Don't force me to do that."

"What do you expect me to say, Max?" I demanded. " 'Okay, thanks a lot, you just go right ahead and slaughter him'? You do what you have to do, and I'll do the same."

Max raised his arms and let them fall. "I have tried."

"Right. But . . ."

"Yes?"

"It goes against the grain," I said. "But—thanks for the warning, Max."

He blinked. "Why don't you go back and get something to eat? It must be close to lunchtime."

"Damned if I will."

"I promise I won't touch him while you are gone."

"No." I sat down, cross-legged. "I want to watch."

Max snapped out an expletive, turned on his heel, and addressed Rudi. "Start walking."

"In which direction, Max?"

Another argument ensued. Max suggested one direction, John another (which Max instantly dismissed), and Georg offered to calculate the spatial errors that would result from a mistaken bearing of five or ten degrees. Finally Max did what I would have done. He told Rudi to use Willy, still rigid as a flagpole in the middle of the pasture, as his focal point, and walk straight toward him. Somewhat to my surprise the resultant path took Rudi along the line John had indicated. When Rudi finished counting, he and Willy were only a few feet apart.

Max looked pleased. "It appears to work. The error is no more than might be expected."

"But your method is riddled with errors," Georg complained, in a pettish tone. "You assume too much; you compound your errors by—"

"Be quiet," Max ordered. "The rest of you—dig."

Up to this point John had been uncharacteristically quiet, his only contributions consisting of brief comments and suggestions. Max hadn't forbidden direct communication, so I said to John, "Are you all right? You look pale."

"Christ, no, I'm not all right. I'm sick."

"Serves you right," Max said, without turning. "Those disgusting eggs of yours have unsettled my stomach as well."

"I could make a delicious stew," John muttered, swaying like a birch in a breeze. "Let me go back and lie down for a bit, Max, and I'll cook—"

"I allowed you to prepare breakfast because I was watching every move you made," was the curt reply. "If you are bored, you can give Hans help with the digging. Your upset stomach will be cured soon enough."

I honestly don't believe he knew what he was doing. It was all part of the day's work to him. But anticipation is agonizing in itself, and offhand references to a man's imminent demise don't settle his nerves. John turned a shade greener, and I said angrily, "Lay off, Max. He's going to pass out."

"No," John said wanly. "Not until I have to."

Max took this as a reference to the moment of permanent collapse that was rapidly approaching, and gave John a sour smile. I suspected another significance, and took due note of the suggestion.

The digging went on apace. I counted heads. The only one of the gang who was missing was Pierre. Leif had disappeared. I had not noticed his absence, which is some indication of my state of nerves. When I asked Max where he was, I was told he had gone to get water. Georg was thirsty.

Thirst wasn't Georg's only problem. He sat staring at his notebook, pretending to make his useless calculations. His fingers were shaking badly. No wonder his mathematics had been inaccurate.

Before long Leif returned, carrying a thermos. He started to offer me the first drink; Georg snatched the cup out of his hands. "What took you so long?" he demanded, wiping dribbles off his chin with his sleeve. "A man could die of thirst before you helped him. Give me more."

Leif obliged, with an apologetic glance at me. Perhaps you should rest for a while, Georg," he suggested.

"The hell with resting. I'm needed here. These morons are digging in the wrong place."

"I think they aren't digging deep enough," I offered.

Max bit his lip. "Dig deeper," he ordered.

As the pit deepened, so did Max's impatience. When Hans, whose excavation techniques were obviously unpracticed, tossed a shovelful of dirt into Max's face, the latter lost his temper.

"Enough, enough," he sputtered, spitting out mud. "This is madness. Smythe—"

"It's around here somewhere," John insisted. "I told you the estimates were rough. What about there? Dig there."

He indicated one of the pits that had been dug the day before. Max sneered. "A naive effort, Smythe. We have explored that area."

"Maybe you didn't dig deep enough," I said.

With a look that eloquently expressed his opinion of my contribution Max thrust a shovel into John's reluctant hands. "You think it is there? You think we did not dig deep enough?"

"I didn't say that," John protested. "She was the one—"

"Dig."

"Max, old chum, I'd love to, but my wrist—"

"Dig!"

The least I could do was add a few more seconds to the

delaying action. John was obviously getting desperate.

"He can't dig with a sprained wrist," I said. "Give me the shovel, John."

We played tug of war, mutually protesting, until Max intervened. John started digging, ostentatiously favoring his right arm. As he deposited the third spadeful to one side, I saw something shine.

Max saw it at the same moment. Our cries blended. "Wait. Stop digging."

The other diggers, sweating even in the chilly air, were happy to assume the order was directed at them. When Max fished the object out of the dirt and held it up, all eyes were upon him. He let out a little hiss of breath and a slow smile curved his lips.

"It appears I did you an injustice, Smythe."

The brooch would be a good three inches in diameter when the crumpled gold was straightened. The tortuous patterns of Anglo-Saxon design formed writhing abstract animal forms around the rim, encircling a rough polished stone. Deep in its garnet depths a sullen glow of crimson glimmered. It was a lovely thing, quite typical of its period. I would have expected nothing less. John dealt with only expert forgers.

I didn't doubt for an instant that John had planted the brooch during the night. I was afraid to look at him. Max was as tickled as a kid who sees a fat, bearded man in a red suit coming down the chimney, after he has decided there is no Santa Claus.

"I told you," John said.

"Get out of the way." Max snatched the shovel from him. In his exuberance he almost went so far as to dig, himself. Recollecting himself in time, he handed the shovel to Rudi. "Carefully," he cautioned. "Carefully."

"Shouldn't use spades," Georg muttered thickly. "Bad technique. Trowels, brushes . . ."

Leif, who had pressed forward as eagerly as the others at the seductive gleam of gold, turned anxiously to his brother.

"Georg, you are not well. Come back to the house. I will help you."

Georg struck his arm aside. "Don't need your help. Leave me alone, damn it." He marched off.

"Maybe you had better go with him," I said.

Leif shook his head. "He is angry with me. I can't help him now. But later—I will take him to a hospital, a sanitarium. They will cure him." He looked at me as if expecting agreement. All I could say was "I hope so."

"They will cure him! He will resume his career, he will succeed. And I will make sure no other devils like this one corrupt him."

He turned to John, who returned his glare with bland indifference. "I wouldn't bank on it, Leif," he said. "Once a junkie, always a junkie."

"I ignore your cheap taunts," Leif said. "You know the saying: He who laughs last . . ."

"Tactless," John said. "Uncouth and tactless, Leif. An honest, law-abiding chap like you shouldn't revel in murder, even mine."

The diggers took the hole down almost six feet before they gave up. They weren't disheartened, however; as Max himself admitted, the treasure trove might have been scattered to some degree. They started another excavation beside the first.

According to my watch, it was after one o'clock. In another nine or ten hours the light would be as dim as it was going to get. I gave the quiescent clouds a critical stare. A good wet, dark, noisy thunderstorm would be a big help.

The discovery of the brooch had whetted appetites that had become jaded, and prolonged the search. Yet I held to my original belief that Max would leave the island that night. There would be no darkness to veil his departure, but the chance of being observed would be lessened if he waited till the townspeople were asleep. He would have to halt the excavation by late afternoon in order to complete his preparations for departure—packing, repairing the boat, killing John—and by that time he would be extremely exasperated, for he would find nothing. There was no treasure trove, at least not in the spot where he was digging—only John's fake brooch.

All of which meant that I didn't dare wait until suppertime to use the contents of the bottle with which John had thoughtfully provided me. His assumption that I would know what it was, and what to do with it, was flattering, but I wished he had taken the time to drop a few hints. I had sneaked a peek at it after breakfast; it was a crystalline white powder with no perceptible odor or other distinguishing characteristics. I didn't taste it. For all I knew, it might be cyanide or some other deadly poison, the slightest nibble of which would send me rolling around the room with my heels touching my head.

I was not keen on the idea of becoming a mass poisoner. However, I thought it unlikely that John would carry a lethal substance around with him. He wasn't the type to swallow cyanide to avoid torture; he'd go on squirming and scheming until the last breath. More likely the powder had come from Georg's pack—coke, heroin, morphine, God knows what. How John had covered up the theft I could not imagine; presumably he had managed to make it look like an accident, or carelessness on Georg's part. Wherever it had originated, it was obviously not meant for my own use, so I had to assume he wanted me to bestow it on the thugs.

Shortly thereafter I was relieved to find my deductions confirmed. John began twitching and clutching his stomach. "I'm in agony," he moaned. "It's probably a ruptured spleen."

"Probably hunger pangs," I said, and was rewarded by a quick glance of approval. I went on, "Maybe Max will let you go back to the house and make yourself a sandwich. You can make one for me while you're at it."

"You'd ask a dying man—a man suffering from extreme inanition—to make you a sandwich?"

"Your playacting is becoming banal, Smythe," Max said. "You read too many sensational novels. It is only in fiction that warders are tricked into carelessness by a pretense of illness."

However, the mention of food had its effect on the diggers. They had been hard at it for several hours, and it was exercise of a type to which they were not accustomed. The wind had dropped to a breathless hush that was more threatening than a gale. Rudi finally summoned up nerve enough to ask Max if they could take a break. "We cannot work all day without food, Max," he added sullenly.

"Don't expect me to do the cooking," John said, between groans.

"Dr. Bliss and I will be the chefs," Max said. "Rudi, take that section down another foot, then stop. Bring Smythe back with you—and watch him."

Max spoke only once during the walk. "I am tempted to lock you in your room this afternoon, Dr. Bliss."

"Why don't you?"

"I cannot trust you," Max explained, in an accusing voice. "You might try to escape."

Any comment on this seemed superfluous. We proceeded in silence.

Though the deep freeze and the pantry shelves were bulging, supplies of perishables like milk and eggs were getting low. The island must have a regular delivery service from the mainland for items of that sort—another reason why time was running out for Max. He couldn't kidnap the milkman and the baker when they made their rounds; someone would wonder what had happened to them. Any visit from an outsider carried the risk of discovery.

I poured the rest of the milk into a pitcher and put it on the table. Max pulled out a chair and sat down. He had no intention of helping me—he just wanted to keep an eye on me. "Sandwiches," he said. "Cheese, ham—nothing complicated."

"We're almost out of bread."

"There is more in the freezer."

"It's frozen solid."

"Then unfreeze it."

I put a couple of loaves in the oven and switched it on. As I moved back and forth between pantry and sink, refrigerator and stove, I had ample opportunity to dispose of the white powder. It would take only a second or two to dump it into—into what? Not the milk; the pitcher was at Max's elbow. Besides, he and Hans were the only members of the gang who drank milk.

"What about some soup?" I suggested. "There's tomato, chicken noodle—"

"No soup."

I don't think he was really worried about my slipping

something into the soup; his objection was pure reflex, instinctive professional caution. Sugar? I thought. No good. Some of them took their coffee black. I plugged in the gleaming chrome-and-porcelain device Mrs. Andersson used for making coffee, and tested the bread. It was pre-sliced; I was able to separate the slices and spread them on the counter to finish thawing. As I did so, I heard voices outside. The diggers were back. I had to make up my mind in a hurry. With all of them milling around the kitchen, my chances of being detected rose a hundredfold.

So I put it in the butter. It was soft, since Max had not let me clear away after breakfast. It also showed signs of having been licked. "Wonderful for hair balls," I said aloud, mixing furiously.

"What did you say?"

"Nothing." If I hadn't been so rattled, I wouldn't have spoken; for all his fondness for animals, Max might be one of those fastidious souls who would refuse to eat food a cat had tasted. The cat had clearly been on the table; there wasn't a scrap of bacon left, and several plates were suspiciously clean.

I started putting the sandwiches together. No self-respecting Swede would have touched them; they were slapped into shape with such speed that the contents leaked over the sides. I took care not to let the butter ooze, though. It was strangely lumpy-looking.

Grimy, sweaty, and disheveled, the diggers filed in and took their places. Hans grabbed a sandwich, and my heart stopped with a grinding thud as he pried back the top piece of bread and peered at what was inside.

"Gibt es keinen Senf?" he inquired.

I didn't trust myself to speak. I got the mustard out of the refrigerator and handed it to him.

It was not one of my more elegant table settings. I

hadn't bothered to put plates down, just a few glasses and a dozen bottles of beer. Hans reached for the pitcher of milk. John got it first, and pulled it toward him. Rudi asked for a bottle opener. Turning to get it, I heard a crash, a splash, and a cry of outrage from Max. John had dropped the pitcher. The milk was soaking into Max's hand-stitched suede shoes.

"Weak wrist," John whined, nursing it.

So everybody drank beer. I made sandwiches like an assembly line. I had to do something; every time one of them took a bite I expected a complaint or a puzzled look.

They had almost finished eating when Leif entered. "Have a sandwich," I said compulsively.

"No, thank you. My brother is ill. We must have a doctor."

Several of the men exchanged cynical grins, but Max looked up sharply. "Ill? What do you mean?"

"I insist you look at him," Leif said. "At once."

His peremptory tone made Max frown, and he added, in a more conciliatory voice, "It may be food poisoning; I cannot tell. Would it not be advisable for you to investigate?"

They went out of the room. The men went right on eating. The suggestion of food poisoning didn't bother them; they had diagnosed Georg's illness sight unseen, and—I thought—correctly. John sat slumped in his chair. He had not touched the sandwiches. I nudged him and offered another plateful.

"Perhaps," I said, "you prefer plain ham."

He took one. Our eyes met for an instant, then he looked away.

Max and Leif came back. I looked up interestedly, but no explanations were forthcoming. Max only said, "Back to work."

There was some subdued grumbling, especially from Hans; five sandwiches and four bottles of beer had not filled his huge stomach. John had to be dragged to his feet. He kept complaining that he was sick, but as he stumbled out, roughly assisted by Hans, Leif said with a contemptuous smile, "His nerve has failed. It was to be expected. He has not even the courage of a cornered rat; he can only cringe and whimper."

I made a protesting sound. Leif's gloating smile faded. "I am sorry, Vicky. But if you could see Georg as he is now, you would understand why I cannot pity the man who corrupted him."

"It's not food poisoning, then?"

"No, I only said that to force Max to look at him. It is— what you think. He has run out of the drug. During the night he neglected to close the box, and it was spilled."

"A little cold turkey," I said meditatively. "Who knows, it may be the making of him."

"Now you sound like that swine Smythe. I hate to hear you so cynical, Vicky."

Max reappeared at the door. "Are you coming?"

"I will stay with my brother," Leif said, in a voice that dared Max to object. "Let her stay too. She is distressed—"

"No, I'll go. I'd rather." I edged away from him.

"You cannot guard him forever," Max said.

The knife was on the counter, an inch from my hand. My fingers itched, but I was afraid to take the chance. I said, "I'm coming, Max. Let's go."

The next hour was the worst of the entire affair. My stomach was churning. I didn't know how long it would take for the powder to work, or what the effects would be—if any. Maybe I had spread it too thin. John sat on the ground, his head bent and his hands limp. I paced, biting my nails. The clouds darkened. The wind rose. The only effect lacking was a werewolf howling in the trees.

I expected Hans to show the first symptoms, since he had eaten and drunk more than the others, but perhaps his mammoth body could absorb more. I saw nothing out of the way until Rudi let out a howl of pain. He had jabbed himself in the foot with his spade. Dropping the tool, he lifted the injured member with one hand and promptly toppled over.

Max was on the spot instantly. "What is it?"

Rudi rolled over, grimacing with pain. "I couldn't help it, Max. I am no laborer. I am exhausted."

Max swept the rest of the crew with a suspicious eye. However, the next to go was not one of his men, it was John. With a startled cry he half rose and then pitched over onto his side.

"Faking," said Max, nudging him with his toe.

A genteel trickle of blood oozed out of John's left nostril. I peeled back one of his eyelids. Now that the time had come, my hands were quite steady.

"He's not faking. Look—dilated pupils, bleeding from the nose. . . . He's got concussion. He'll die if he doesn't get help."

"I will, of course, send one of my men for a doctor immediately," Max said, with awful sarcasm. "Do be sensible, my dear. It is a far easier death than the one he faced."

"At least let me do what I can," I begged. "Lying on the cold ground like that . . ." I peeled off my sweater and tucked it around John. "Give me your coat," I said.

"Don't be ridiculous, Dr. Bliss."

"Please . . ." I rose and approached the diggers. A couple of them looked a little dazed. "Please," I repeated. "He needs to be kept warm."

It was Hans, the big, good-natured oaf, who responded. "I am too warm," he mumbled. "You can have my sweater." He did look warm. Perspiration beaded his forehead.

In the last split second I made a final check of the dispositions I had noted earlier. A man can't dig and hold a gun at the same time. Three of them wore shoulder holsters, including Max. Rudi's weapon—a cute little sawed-off shotgun—was on the wheelbarrow, atop the other tools. I waited until Hans had the sweater up over his head before I acted. My shrill, banshee scream stunned them for another essential second. It also told John that I was making my move.

The only one whose hand made it to the butt of his gun was the swarthy Italian. I aimed at him. In case he suffered from delusions about the incompetence of the female, I said warningly, "I was brought up on a farm, boys. Don't chance it."

There were no heroes in that crowd. Any such aspirations died when they realized mine wasn't the only weapon pointing at them. Max was on the ground, out cold, and John had his gun.

He wasted no time complimenting me. After he had relieved the men of their surplus armaments, he gestured at Max. "Pick him up."

The order was directed at Hans, but that unfortunate innocent was still hopelessly entangled in the folds of his sweater. His pale-blue eyes peered over it with vague wonder.

Rudi and Willy carried Max. They were all looking groggy. The combination of beer and dope hadn't knocked them out, but it had slowed their reflexes just enough to make the crazy plan feasible. Urged by guns and exhortations, the procession made its way to the hut in the trees. It took John only a few seconds to open the padlock, with the heavy needles in my pocket sewing kit. He bundled the prisoners inside and snapped the lock. Then, for the first time, he addressed me.

"Where is Gus?"

"The barn. I thought you were supposed to look for him."

"I had too many other things to do last night. Besides, I knew you wouldn't take my word for it."

He had a point. I said, "Hadn't we better collect the rest of the artillery?"

"Yes, right. We can't carry that lot around; it's too bulky. Over the cliff?"

"Sounds good to me—" I broke off with a gulp. The figure looming up in front of me looked like an ambulatory tree trunk, featureless against the lighter gray of the open pasture beyond.

"Vicky! Thank heaven, you are all right. I heard you scream; I thought . . ." Leif held out his arms. I stayed where I was.

"Put your hands up, Hasseltine," John said, edging away.

"Don't be afraid." Leif's voice was contemptuous. "I would not risk myself for you, but I am happy you have succeeded. Now I can take my brother to a doctor. Come, let us return to the house."

Not unnaturally, he kept an eye on John's gun, turning as the latter continued to move sideways. The muzzle of the weapon stayed fixed on Leif's chest, and he said impatiently, "Don't be a fool, Smythe. Vicky, convince him that I—"

I hit him across the side of the head with the barrel of the shotgun. He had a skull like a granite boulder. The blow dropped him to his knees, but he didn't flatten out until John had pounded him a few more times, with the methodical precision of a carpenter driving in spikes.

"That's enough," I said, wincing.

John handed me the gun.

"Keep him covered," he said.

Kneeling, he yanked off his belt and strapped Leif's ankles. I contributed my belt, which he used on Leif's wrists. He wasn't satisfied. "What we need is a drum of wire," he grumbled. "Go get that heavy twine Georg was using, and be quick about it."

By the time he finished, Leif had begun to stir and mutter.

"Shall we put him in the shed?" I asked.

"Can you think of any reason why we should open that door?"

"Actually, I can think of several good reasons why we shouldn't. Let's go."

Chapter Ten

IT DIDN'T TAKE long to dispose of the extraneous weapons, but John begrudged every second. He was moving with the eellike quickness he displayed when the bad guys were breathing down his neck. He didn't have to spell it out for me. We had the upper hand, but only temporarily. The only way of immobilizing a crowd like that permanently is with a machine gun. Our insane coup had succeeded because we caught them off guard and hustled them into prison before they had time to realize how vulnerable we were. The shack wouldn't hold them forever; and the odds were almost four to one against us —higher, considering that they were trained killers, that Max might have a reserve supply of artillery in his luggage, and that Leif was an army in himself. I could picture him snapping his bonds like a comic-book hero bursting out of his shirt when he turns into Captain Muscle. There

was no need for a consultation on our next move. We had
to go, and stay not upon the order of our going. I had no
idea how we were going to get off the island, but when
push came to shove I'd have preferred to take my chances
in the water rather than huddle in a cul-de-sac with Leif
on my trail.

For all his quickness, John was not at his best. When we
started back across the pasture toward the house, his
breathing was a little too fast.

"We work so well together," he remarked. "It almost
smacks of clairvoyance—the marriage of true minds."

"You needn't be insulting."

That shut him up for a while. Then he said, "How did
you know Leif was one of them?"

"Anything you can figure out, I can figure out. Or did
you know already?"

"No. I knew Max must be taking orders from someone,
and toward the end he was making decisions a little too
quickly; there wasn't time for him to have communicated
with a distant headquarters. He also got careless about
guarding Hasseltine."

"Right."

"Right, you say. I'll wager it was good old feminine
intuition."

I didn't answer. His hit came too close to the mark.

My discovery had been based on logical reasoning;
Leif's performance, as Swedish cop and as German engineer, had been discordant with sour notes. His suitcase
was the giveaway. He could have swum the lake, but not
with that heavy bag. I hadn't thought it out so neatly,
though; it had all come together in a wave of instinctive
revulsion when Leif made love to me, a dreadful illusion
that the hands moving over my body were sticky and
slippery with blood—the hands of a killer.

The clouds spit out a windy gust of rain and closed up again. We reached the grove of trees behind the barnyard and John said, "Hold on a minute. I want to say something."

His voice sounded odd. I turned. He clung for support to one of the pale birch trunks, his chest rising and falling rapidly. In the gloom his tumbled hair had a silvery luster.

"It's okay," I said gruffly. "You don't have to thank me."

"I wasn't about to."

"Well, you damned well should! I didn't have to stick my neck out for you! In fact, any woman with the brains of a louse would have helped Max beat you up last night."

"He had plenty of help."

After a moment I said, "Leif?"

"He didn't join in. He just watched. And made a few suggestions."

"That was careless of him."

"Not really. He's so rotten with conceit he assumed you wouldn't believe me even if I had a chance to accuse him. It was," John said thoughtfully, "becoming more and more difficult for him to restrain himself. His feelings for Georg are the closest he can come to normal human emotions. Unluckily for me . . . Luckily for me, and you, his passion for revenge made him careless. He's up to his neck in this affair; the police may just manage to pin it on him."

"Did you know Georg was his brother?"

"Good God, no. I wouldn't have touched that deal with the proverbial ten-foot pole if I had realized the hairy degenerate was related to one of the top men in the business. Blood will tell, though; long before I ran into him, Georg had picked up some of the tricks of the trade, despite Leif's efforts to keep him legitimate."

"Bless your heart," I said. "I might have known you

wouldn't turn a nice innocent boy on to drugs."

"I avoid that aspect of organized crime," was the austere reply. "It lacks class."

"So what do we do now?"

His hair was speckled with dirt and twigs; the trickle of dried blood under his nose looked like a sloppily trimmed mustache. "I rather hoped you would have an idea," he said.

"I haven't had time to think, dammit. The only way of dealing with a chaotic situation like this one is to grab the opportunities as they come up; it's impossible to plan in advance."

"I didn't ask for a lecture, darling, or for a list of excuses. Hans can probably demolish that shack board by board in a couple of hours. I plan to be miles away by that time."

"We could call for help."

"Fine, if you happen to have a shortwave hidden in your lingerie. Or shall we all stand on the shore and shout?"

"Max may have a radio somewhere."

"If he has, I haven't found it, and I assure you, I looked. Besides, I don't fancy cowering in the cellar waiting for possibly hypothetical help to arrive. Max might decide to fire the house."

"Maybe Gus will have a suggestion."

"We can certainly ask," John said. "All right, let's get him out. What do you propose to do about the guard?"

"I read a book once where the heroine took off her clothes and walked into the room where the villains were—"

"Don't be vulgar."

The only tricky part was locating Pierre, who had taken shelter in the garden shed. In the end I had to call him.

When he saw me, smiling and innocent and unarmed, he came out, and John took care of the rest. We tied him up with Georg's twine and tossed him back into the shed, wedging the door with a log from the woodpile.

The barn door was held by a bar so big it took both of us to lift it out of the massive iron staples. When it swung open, the smell struck me motionless with nostalgia; no matter how much you clean, you can never dispel the old ghosts of manure, hay, and warm animal bodies. It smelled marvelous.

It was lucky for me that I stopped. The heavy stick whistled through the air, missing my nose by a few inches.

"Wait, Gus—" Before I could go on, I was enveloped in a rib-cracking hug. "Vicky, my dear child—have I hurt you? I dared not wait any longer, I feared for your life—"

"It's okay. But we've got to get away, Gus, as fast as we can."

Gus let me go and turned to John, who was watching with a fixed, ingratiating smile. Before I could speak or move, Gus raised his fist and brought it crashing down on John's head. He crumpled up like a piece of aluminum guttering.

I caught Gus's arm. "Don't. He's on our side."

"My poor Vicky, you are mistaken," Gus said seriously. "He has a gun, don't you see? And I must tell you that he is not kin to us. It is impossible that Great-great-aunt Birgitta could have—"

"I know, I know, I know. Actually, he's—never mind, it would take too long to explain. Just take my word for it."

I knelt and tried to straighten John's tangled limbs. This had not been his day. "Wake up," I said, shaking him.

"Not until you convince Cousin Gus," said John, without opening his eyes.

"He's convinced. Right, Gus?" I grabbed John's collar and dragged him to his feet. He stood swaying, head on one side, like Petrouchka, in the ballet of the same name.

"If you say so," Gus agreed doubtfully. "Where are the other evil men?"

"Locked up."

"Temporarily." John straightened, with some effort. "I fear this isn't the time to break out the champagne, Mr. Jonsson. You wouldn't happen to have an extra boat hidden away?"

"Only in the boathouse," Gus said. "We must telephone to the police. . . . No. They have cut the wires?"

"And smashed your shortwave."

"Then one of us must go for help." Gus flexed his arms and shoulders. I had to admire the quickness with which his mind worked; he had considered and comprehended the possibilities before I could explain them. He went on, "They would also immobilize the boats, yes. Very well. I shall swim to the other side. Vicky will lock herself in the cellar with the gun, and you to protect her. . . ."

"Or vice versa," said John, as Gus studied him dubiously. "Tell him, Vicky. He seems to lack confidence in me."

Looking at Gus, I almost believed he could do it. John was the subject of my concern now. The last blow on the head hadn't done him any good. He caught my eye and grinned, in the old mocking fashion.

"I'd prefer to take my chances with Mother Nature," he said. "Maybe we won't have to swim. Come along."

Another spatter of rain struck stingingly into my face as we crossed the barnyard. Thunder rumbled distantly.

A shaft of light streaked the sky to the north.

"Did you see that?" I grabbed John's arm.

He let out a hiss of pain and shook me off. "What?"

"Lightning. Only it wasn't. Thunder comes after the flash, not before."

"Flashlight?"

"Looked like it."

"Damn. I thought we'd have more time."

"Tell me what to do," Gus said calmly.

"Run," John said, and set the example.

After hanging coyly around all day, the storm had made up its mind to move in. Lightning wove patterns jagged as the designs on Celtic goldwork across the tarnished silver of the sky. The rain began in earnest as we approached the garden; within seconds I was soaked to the skin, and water was running down the path like a little river. Gus hobbled like the Hunchback of Notre Dame, but he hobbled fast, and he was more surefooted than I on the steep wooden stairs.

John slammed the boathouse doors and barred them. It was almost as dark as midnight inside, but John has eyes like a cat's; as Gus moved toward the switch, he snapped, "No lights. Let them look for us."

"I have a flashlight," I said.

"I knew you would. Keep it down, away from the window."

Gus swore extensively in Swedish when he saw the havoc wrought among his boats. When John grunted, "Give me a hand, you two," we helped tug at the rowboat's painter. I had forgotten how heavy a waterlogged boat can be; it seemed to take forever to haul it up onto the deck. John groped under one of the seats and fished out a roll of some material that shone greasily in the narrow beam of the flashlight.

"Mr. Jonsson, get ready to open the outer doors," he said.

I watched in mounting disbelief as he spread the piece of leather over the hole in the bottom of the boat. It looked like—it surely was—the side of a calfskin suitcase.

"Oars," John said to me.

"I'd rather swim."

"You may have to."

"John, that won't—"

"It's waterlogged and somewhat adhesive. One of us will have to sit on it, that's all. And bail like hell."

He grabbed a can from the shelves and gave it to me. I gave it back. "You sit, you bail like hell. Where are the damned oars? Oh—I've got them."

"Ready," Gus called.

"Okay, open up. Lights out, Vicky." Before I pressed the switch, I saw John lower himself into the boat. His face was screwed up like that of a man expecting to get hit with a pie.

"Well," he said, out of the darkness, "it hasn't sunk yet. Hop in."

I had a brief argument with Gus, who wanted to do the rowing. I took one oar, he took the other. After a nerve-racking false start we got into the rhythm, and the boat shot out into open water. Gus laughed with pure pleasure. "What is the phrase—a chip off the old block?"

I would have acknowledged the compliment, but the full force of the waves hit just then, and we had to do some fancy rowing to keep from being swamped. I let Gus do most of the work, for he was the expert, following his orders mechanically. After a few frenzied moments he had us heading into the wind. John bailed like a madman, but there was a lot of water sloshing around in the bottom, and the boat's response to the oars was unpleasantly sluggish.

Still, it was better than swimming, if hardly less wet, and a great deal better than playing games with Leif and Max. The storm was directly overhead now; thunder boomed like a bass drum arpeggio, the rain was an icy shower, lightning ripped the dark apart. In between thunderclaps I heard John swearing as he bailed. The water seemed to be coming in faster than he threw it out. I didn't care. I was filled with a crazy exhilaration that brushed aside the weather, the leaky boat, and the ache across my shoulder blades as I bent and straightened in time with Gus. He was as fey as I; he started to sing in a reverberant baritone. I assumed from the rhythm that it was a classic Swedish boating song, so I joined in with "Speed, bonnie boat, like a bird on the wing. . . ."

The rain began to slacken. A finger of paler gray parted the clouds. The boat moved like a dying animal, but my wild spirits refused to be squelched. We were all right now. Even if the boat sank, we could make it. In a few minutes we'd be in Gus's warm, dry car, speeding along the road to the town.

"Loud the winds blow," I sang, "loud the waves—"

He came up out of the water in a great soaring leap, like a demonic creature half-fish and half-man. Water streaming from his hair and body surrounded him with a ghastly green glow of phosphorescence.

My voice rose to a high note that is not part of "The Skye Boat Song." The others hadn't seen him; Gus was staring soulfully at the storm, and John was bent over bailing. My shriek alerted them in time to observe Leif's next appearance. He was on the same side of the boat— my side. He moved in the choppy water as if it were his natural element, perfectly at ease, smiling. . . . One bronzed arm lifted and came down, delicately, gently. A beaded line of blood sprang up across the back of my hand, blurring as it spread.

Leif went under. The boat dipped; water began trickling in over the gunwales. Not much water—he didn't want us to sink, not before we had plenty of time to think about what was going to happen to us.

John brought the bailing can down on the whitened fingers that curled over the side. They disappeared, and the boat lifted sluggishly. We turned in a slow, reluctant circle as I freed my oar. It was the only thing I could think of to do, but I was well aware it was a futile gesture. The oar was too unwieldy to use as a club, especially since my quarry would probably not be considerate enough to stay in one spot so I could brain him. The gun was no use, it was in my purse, which was six inches under water, in the bottom of the boat.

John kept spinning around on his backside. If he got up, the ineffectual patch would give way altogether and we would sink like a stone. I figured we were going to sink anyway. It wouldn't have been a disaster if Leif had not been lying in wait like the Loch Ness monster. He was unencumbered by bulky clothing—that sleek, shining torso, limned by pale fire, was a sight I would never forget. John was hurt and Gus was crippled, and with his handy knife Leif could pick us off one by one before we reached shore.

The sky lightened rapidly. I saw the hand the next time it appeared, and since it was—of course—on my side, I bent over and bit it. The boat was rocking, water was coming in from every possible direction, and Gus was flailing around with his oar. If Leif didn't sink us, he would. Under the sound of water and Gus's infuriated bellows I heard a confused roaring noise, which I took to be the pounding of my overstrained heart.

Leif came up again, treading water. He slashed at my hand and slipped sideways as Gus struck at him with the oar. Another blurring crimson line crossed the first on the back of my hand. *X* marks the spot? Half of a double-cross? The specific reference was obscure, but the general meaning was clear. I was now number one on Leif's hate list, and he wanted me to know it. A slash here and a slash there, weakening, demoralizing—once in the water, I'd be easy prey for a murderous merman.

John rose to his knees. Somehow during the chaos he had managed to strip off shoes and sweater. One vigorous yank pulled most of the buttons off his shirt, and he shrugged out of it as I made an ineffective attempt to grab him. I think he said something, but I'm not sure. He slid over the side, leaving his pants floating on the surface until the water soaked them and they sank, with gruesome slowness.

There was no sound except that distant roaring. The water poured in. Gus was pulling at me, trying to get between me and the sleek fishlike shape that kept leaping and slashing, leaping and slashing. I couldn't move. Blood poured down my arm and hand, but it wasn't physical weakness that held me paralyzed, it was superstitious terror. Leif's monstrous form seemed more, or less, than human, a water demon, an aquatic Bane.

He came up again, right beside me. His face was only inches from mine. His lips were drawn back in a fixed grin and his eyes were flat as brown glass. A ray of feeble sunlight glinted off the knife blade.

The valiant, abused craft finally gave way. But just before the icy water took me, I saw Leif's grin vanish and a look of mingled fury and disbelief transform his face as he was pulled down into the steel-gray depths.

I swallowed a couple of pints of water before I managed to fight my way back to the surface. Somehow I was not at all surprised to find myself in the solicitous grasp of a total stranger whose face was blackened like Al Jolson's.

---

ii

So, after all, I danced the maypole dance with the people of Karlsholm on Midsummer Day.

I wore a dress that had belonged to Gus's wife, brilliant with embroidery and laced with silver chains. Fortunately for me, she had been a stout, healthy woman, but we had to add a ruffle on the skirt. That was no problem for the housewives of Karlsholm. They'd have embroidered a whole dress if I had let them.

My partner was Erik, the son of Gus's chauffeur; he steered me through the dance so adeptly that I didn't screw up the pattern more than five or six times. Gus watched from the sidelines. He occupied the chair of honor, under a bower of green branches. When I glanced in his direction, which I did every time I went around the circle, he smiled and waved. He was trying to help me forget my tragedy. From time to time he addressed a remark to the little bald man beside him. The two of them had struck up quite a friendship.

But I guess I had better recapitulate.

The commando who hauled me out of the lake handed me over to a circle of waiting arms. To my dazed eyes the crowd seemed to number in the hundreds—more commandoes with blackened faces, mingling familiarly with elderly housewives and sedate old gentlemen in their Sunday best and sturdy youths wearing jeans. I fought my way out of a smothering mass of sympathetic faces.

"Please—let me go back—he's still out there. . . ." They wouldn't let me go, they kept crooning at me and holding on. My muscles had gone soggy, so I couldn't break away, and I couldn't understand a word of the soft litany, but I knew what they were saying—oh, yes, I knew. . . .

After an eon Gus came limping into the throng, pushing people gently aside until we stood face to face. His hair and clothes were soaked. Water trickled down his cheeks.

"My child," he said, and held out his hands.

I don't make a habit of fainting, but this seemed like a suitable moment for it.

iii

They took Leif out of the water later that evening. I didn't see him, but I heard people talking. I suppose the citizens of Karlsholm are still talking about him. Beautiful as Baldur, mighty as Thor . . . The water hadn't damaged him, but there were deep slashes across his arms and chest.

They found no other bodies, though they searched for hours.

I frustrated the good ladies of the village by refusing to stay in bed. Why should I? I felt fine. I had the second-best guestroom in the mayor's house—the best, despite his protests, was reserved for Gus—and we spent the evening in the mayoral parlor, waiting for the police to arrive. There was enough food to feed a regiment and enough drink to drive us into permanent alcoholism and two dozen people trying to explain what had been going on. The mayor's wife finally won out, since she combined the loudest voice with the most idiomatic English. I summarize.

"Mrs. Andersson knew something was wrong. It was not like Mr. Jonsson to send everyone away, on such short notice, and Mrs. Andersson, who has read many detective stories, was sure the little gray man had a pistol under his coat. She saw the bulge. She said nothing and pretended to suspect nothing for fear the gray man would hurt Mr. Jonsson. When she came here, with the others, we sat down and tried to think what to do. The police? *Ya,* the police are very well, but we feared they would attack, with guns and boats, and you would all be murdered. They could do nothing we could not do as well."

She may have been right about that. Most of the men, and some of the women, had done their military training, and all of them were totally at home in the water. The island had been under observation from the first, by watchers hidden among the trees and by the petrified old gentlemen on the dock. They had seen me come and go, but had never caught a glimpse of Gus, and their anxiety mounted until it was decided they could wait no longer.

The operation had been mounted with typical Swedish thoroughness. The raid was supposed to take place that night, but one of the watchers on the east side of the lake had seen our activities in the pasture. He couldn't make out exactly what was going on, but he didn't like the looks of things, so the rescuers got ready to move in. Because of the foul weather they didn't see us till we were close to shore. During the frenzied seconds while Leif had tried to sink us we had been under observation by dozens of horrified eyes. That was the part I found hardest to believe—that the seemingly interminable interlude had happened so fast that the rescuers were unable to react, much less interfere, until it was almost over. I hadn't even noticed them. I wondered if John had. . . .

Mrs. Mayor had seen him go over the side. She was one

of the few watchers who had the presence of mind to keep her binoculars trained on Leif instead of being distracted by the capsized boat. Her description made the struggle sound like a Norse epic—flailing arms, struggling bodies, foam-lashed water, and the slow spreading stain on the surface. . . .

When she got to that point, Gus let out a mammoth cough and stamped on her foot. She shut up, with a guilty look at me. Actually, the spreading bloodstain was probably her own invention. I doubt she could see it from so far away, even though the weather had cleared.

The realization of her tactlessness silenced the poor lady, and her husband had to finish the story.

"We had our plans made. Ten of our best young men. Knives they took, but no other weapons. The villains must be overpowered in silence. We had one of them, in the cell in the town hall—"

"What?" I demanded. "One of whom?"

"Ya, he came the same day, after Mrs. Andersson had told us of the danger, so we were ready for him." The mayor beamed. "He thought to deceive us. We are not so easily fooled, no. He said he was a friend of the lady's. Ha! We lock him up, then we also have a hostage. Now, soon, all his criminal friends will join him in the prison."

I almost hated to ask. "What does he look like, this villain?"

"Oh, a harmless little man in his looks. It is always so with villains, ja? Stout, with a round, smiling face . . ."

I stood up and stretched. I was wearing one of Mrs. Mayor's flannel robes, which went around me twice and barely reached my calves, but I decided against changing. The more pathetic I looked, the easier it would be to calm him.

"You had better let me see this villain," I said.

I don't know what Schmidt had to complain about. The "cell" in the town hall, which also served as youth center, cinema, social club, and anything else necessary, was a pleasant room with a comfortable bed and pots of flowers on the windowsills. They had fed him regularly and let him keep his suitcase, which—typically—contained one change of clothing, two ponderous scholarly tomes, and four pornographic novels. But the way that man carried on, you'd have thought he had spent twenty-four hours hanging by his thumbs in a dungeon full of rats.

I let him get it out of his system, and then, as I had expected, he hugged me and told me I looked terrible. "Poor girl, what you have been through! But it is your own fault. If you had confided in me . . . I have been so worried for your safety! And it serves you right; you will never learn to trust others."

There were a few more fading rumbles of complaint before Schmidt dropped into a chair and mopped his face. "Sit down," he ordered. "Tell me everything."

He said afterwards that it was almost as good as a chapter from my book. Almost. I knew very well what was lacking, but did not feel obliged to pander in the first person to Schmidt's perversions.

He didn't press me. In fact, when I told him, briefly and impersonally, of the denouement, his faded blue eyes filled with tears. Schmidt is very sentimental. He cries over everything, especially corny old German love songs.

"It was the man you knew in Rome?" he asked gently. "Yes."

"My child, time will heal your grief. There are many who love you, who will comfort you—"

"Skip the violins, Schmidt. He dragged me into this."

"But he did not mean to. When he realized the danger,

he tried to save you. And," Schmidt went on, reverting to his familiar grievance, "you had not sense enough to do as he said. If you had returned home, or asked for my help, instead of keeping me always in the dark like a stupid old grandpa. . . . It was your fault."

On the whole, I prefer Schmidt's scoldings to his disgusting wallows in bathos, so I said provocatively, "You can't blame me for your being here. I should have known when I talked to Gerda and got the well-known runaround that you had done some damn-fool thing like haring off to Stockholm."

Schmidt grinned from ear to ear with reminiscent pride. "You did not see me, did you? Not ever! I was following you everywhere. I have not lost the touch. You think I am too old and too fat, but not once did you see Papa Schmidt when he was on the trail."

"And a fat lot of good it did me."

"If you had stayed in Stockholm, I would have helped," Schmidt said angrily. "But no, you must go rushing into the wilderness. I could not find where you had gone. I rented a car, I was lost, many times, many times. . . ."

"You must not speak to her that way," said Gus, from the door.

I introduced the two, adding, "We always yell at each other, Gus. Schmidt is one of my oldest and dearest friends, and I would not deny that he has a point."

"Yes, he is right to scold you for doing foolish things," Gus said. He took a chair next to Schmidt's, and the two of them stared at me with matching expressions of stern disapprobation.

I wondered what local deity I had offended to incur such a curse. Most heroines (in which category I account myself, of course) pick up handsome, dashing heroes as they pass through their varied adventures. I seemed to be building up a collection of critical grandpas.

Schmidt, being the more sentimental of the two, was the first to remember my bereavement. His eyes got watery again.

"We must not scold her now," he said to Gus.

Gus nodded. "You are right. She must not be alone. We will show her how much she is treasured by us."

"It is very romantic," Schmidt assured me. A tear trembled on his eyelid, as if terrified by the vast pink expanse of cheek below, then took the plunge. "You have redeemed this man, my dear. His love for you turned him from his path of crime. He died a hero, saving the life of the woman he loved. Let that comfort you, and let the memory of his gallant death shine in your thoughts through the years of—"

"Shut up, Schmidt," I snarled.

The two heads turned, like Tweedledum and Tweedledee, and nodded solemnly in tempo.

"She is distraught," Schmidt said.

"She does not know what she says," Gus agreed.

What was the use of trying to explain? They wouldn't understand. On the surface the whole affair had been a succession of simple clichés; but motives are never so simple. I didn't even understand my own.

After the first few hours I was pretty sure Gus and I weren't in danger of being killed. Crazy as it may sound, I believed Max. I don't know why; maybe it was the cat that convinced me I could trust his word. Even after I realized that Leif was one of the gang, I wasn't afraid for myself. He'd have let me survive, as the latest of what was undoubtedly a long list of infatuated dupes; his vanity was so overweening that he couldn't believe I had penetrated his disguise until I hit him over the head with it—literally.

I could have played along. It would have been the safest and most sensible course. I owed John nothing. And the funniest thing about it, the thing nobody would believe —except John himself—was that I had not risked myself because I was in love with him. I had always known John for what he was—a corrupt, unscrupulous man with the morals of a tomcat—and I'm not referring to the cat's sexual habits, but to its incurable tendency to put its own interests ahead of everyone else's. I didn't love that man; I didn't even like him. The one I loved was the guy with the perverse sense of humor and the peculiar brand of courage and the occasional streak of quixotry and the clever, twisty mind. But that man was part of the other, buried so deep it was hard to be certain he existed.

I caught a glimpse of him in those last few seconds, just before John went over the side. That was why I tried to stop him. He must have realized, as I did, that I was Leif's primary target. He stood a good chance of getting away while Leif was busy with me. He had a bad arm and a bad head and he was half Leif's size, but he hadn't made a break for it. If he had, I might not have lived to hear Schmidt blathering on about heroic sacrifices and heroic deaths. Is it any wonder I snarled at poor old sentimental Schmidt?

iv

The police had no trouble rounding up the gang. They were not unarmed—Max had another suitcase of weaponry tucked away—but resistance to the death was not part of their credo. With their connections they'd be out on parole in a couple of years, and back at the old stand.

Max asked to see me before they hauled him off to jail.

Schmidt and Gus wanted to go along, to protect me, and I had to be very firm with them.

He rose with his usual courtesy when I entered the room.

"I am glad to see you are unharmed by your adventures," he said. "I felt a certain concern."

"You had cause." I waved him back into his chair. "I suppose I should commiserate with you, but I'm damned if I feel any regret about Leif—Hasseltine—whatever his name."

"It was a business association," Max said calmly. There wasn't a wrinkle in his well-cut suit, his tie was neatly knotted, and his wig was firmly in place; he was the very image of a respectable businessman. "In fact," he added thoughtfully, "his—er—premature demise opens several promising avenues of speculation for me. I might even say, Dr. Bliss, that if you should ever have occasion to call on me for a favor . . ."

I ought to have been shocked and disgusted. But there was something about Max. . . . His composure was so complete that he forced you to accept his premises—for the moment, anyway.

"Thanks," I said. "Was that all you wanted to say?"

"Only to express my personal regrets for the inconvenience you experienced, and to give you this."

They had let him keep his briefcase. From it he took a piece of cardboard and handed it to me. The black silhouette had been neatly mounted.

"I did it from memory," Max said, as I studied the familiar profile. "It is good of him, don't you think?"

"You always do good work, Max. I appreciate it. Did you make another—for your collection?"

"No," Max said deliberately. "No, Dr. Bliss."

I said, "I understand."

"I felt sure you would. May I say, then, good fortune to you, and *auf Wiedersehen.*"

"I sincerely hope not," I said. "Good-bye, Max."

_____**V**

And that, dear reader, is how I came to be footing it, not too lightly, around the Karlsholm maypole. It was an event I wouldn't have missed, a memory I will always cherish. And I'll be back. By dint of desperate searching and ingenious invention, Gus and I worked out a genealogy that made me his fourteenth cousin twice removed, or something of that nature. Kinfolks have to keep in touch. Besides, Schmidt had been working on Gus to permit excavation of the pasture, and Gus was showing signs of yielding.

When the dance ended, I went to join the two of them. They broke off their solemn conversation to offer me a chair and food and drink. Then Gus said hesitantly, "We were speaking of a matter—"

"No, Gus," Schmidt interrupted. "The wound is only beginning to heal. You will rend it open again."

"Shut up, Schmidt," I said.

"I think it will comfort her," Gus answered. "My dear Cousin Vicky, I wish to raise a stone to the memory of the brave man who gave his life for us. Here, on the shore, or on the headland in front of the house—we have not decided."

"How about outside the bedroom windows?" I suggested.

They were used to my frivolous comments; they had

decided to treat them as instances of stiff upper lip.

"We have been discussing the epitaph," Schmidt said. "I favor something like *Dulce et decorum est—*'"

"'To die for one's country'? Not too appropriate, Schmidt."

"But it sounds so well in Latin."

"It is all wrong," Gus insisted. "There is a verse in the Bible—in English it is like this: 'Greater love hath no man. . . .'"

"Something from Shakespeare," Schmidt exclaimed. "He is full of excellent quotations, and what could be more fitting for an English nobleman than the great English poet?"

They went on arguing. Neither of them really gave a damn for my opinion, and I didn't offer it. They would have been scandalized at the quotation I favored as most apropos.

I couldn't be absolutely certain; but Max shared my doubts, and Max knew him well. The opportunity had been too good to pass up—a chance to vanish in a cloud of glory, avoiding awkward questions that might be asked by unsentimental parties on shore, such as the police and the surviving members of Leif's organization. Nobody but me had seen any significance in the disappearance of certain articles of old clothing from Axel Foger's storage shed. In the confusion and excitement of that eventful evening, things were bound to be mislaid.

"Of his bones are coral made?" Not bloody likely. But it reminded me of another quotation from the great English poet—from the same play, in fact. John would have been the first to appreciate it.

"He hath no drowning mark upon him; his complexion is perfect gallows."